Bumfuzzle and Cattywampus:
Unlikely Detectives

Trouble at the Buckeye Festival

Alice Kanaka

Copyright 2023 by Alice Kanaka
Published by author.

ISBN: 979-8-9863105-7-2
First printing March 2023
Cover art by Neutronboar
Edited by Teresa Grabs

Table of Contents

Chapter 1

Preparations for the annual Buckeye Festival were in full swing in the small, midwestern town of Buckwood. Volunteers cheerfully set up canopies and judging tables for homemade hats and baskets, jam, jewelry, and locally grown produce. Children ran through the crowd, sneaking candy and shrieking with joy; dogs barked gleefully as they splashed in the pond. The central park, known to locals as 'the green,' took up three square blocks in the middle of downtown and was bordered by narrow streets, separating it from the surrounding shops and historic civic buildings. Within the park, a construction crew busily completed the large, temporary stage and travelling carnies hastily set up their rides. Food trucks parked in their designated area and rows of arcade games popped up as if by magic.

Standing off to one side of the frenetic activity, sixty-something best friends, Marge Bumfuzzle and Joey Cattywampus, observed the somewhat controlled chaos and enjoyed the crisp autumn day. Marge's yellow and orange polyester pantsuit and enormous carrot-red bun caught the sun and glowed like the autumn foliage. Wearing a western hat and bolo tie, Joey leaned on his crooked walker and surveyed the results of their effort. Even Marge's cat, Fluster, had made an appearance and was currently attempting to climb Sergeant Peter Locke's pantleg. Claws extended, he made his vertical ascent to Peter's head, knocking off his cap, swatting his face with his fluffy tail, and yowling like the world was ending.

"Aunt Marge! Help!"

Marge quickly approached her nephew to assist but was distracted as a young girl skipped through the judging area with a basket, strewing something on the tables she passed.

There was a brief pause as Greg Smithers, the middle-aged Protestant pastor, pushed his square, black glasses higher and strode forward to check the tabletops. Mayhem ensued before he could reach the tables, however, as every dog in the park smelled bacon and came running, jostling the pastor out of the way in the process.

Big dogs, little dogs, fat dogs, skinny dogs; they jumped on tables or pulled on cloths, smashing hats, breaking jars, and squashing tomatoes. Entrants who had spent the year preparing their wares were distraught. Seventy-year-old Millicent Beaumonde was in tears, and the little girl disappeared into the fray. When the stampede died down, everyone present stood and gaped, shocked by the wreckage.

"Fluster, how did you know?" Marge gently disengaged him from Peter's head. "You need some first aid, Petey."

"Who was that child?" Peter winced at the damage Fluster had inflicted upon his person, scratching his leg through his uniform.

"I didn't recognize her, but she looked about four, had blonde pigtails, and was wearing a summery dress."

"I noticed her pink Converse high tops and roll-over socks," Joey added.

Peter placed a call on his radio and pulled out his notebook. "I'll see you later, Aunt Marge," he said as he walked toward the victims of what would later be called the great bacon fiasco.

As Marge and Joey left the tent, Fluster in tow, they ran into Reginald Beaumonde, Millicent's son-in-law. The Beaumonde family lived atop the town's single hill and was as close as Buckwood came to landed gentry. Reginald, who had married into the family and taken their name, affected a jovial bonhomie when he deemed it necessary, but was most often arrogant and condescending toward the townsfolk. Tall and well-built, he brushed by Marge and Joey dismissively.

Marge whispered, "He reeks of bacon."

"They might have had it for breakfast."

"Cooking doesn't create a strong scent that clings. Well, unless someone toils relentlessly in a fast-food kitchen. Reginald smells like he was rolling in it. We must inspect their house for clues."

"It might be too late. Wouldn't he have brought all of it?"

"Perhaps, but an attempt is required. We could ostensibly visit Millicent to see how she's coping with the destruction of her crafts."

Joey nodded. "Are we going to Bible study tonight? I'm feeling a little tired after all this activity."

"It has been an eventful day. Why don't you take your repose while I prepare dinner, then we can discuss how to proceed."

Lost in thought, the ten-minute walk home passed quickly, and Marge looked up in surprise when Joey came to a stop in front of her house. "Will an hour be adequate? I'll telephone Pastor Greg."

"Yes. Sorry to abandon you. Perhaps an hour and a half."

Marge nodded and smiled as she watched him cross the street. Turning, she greeted Fluster, who was sitting impatiently on the porch, then let herself into the house. She almost called to Joey that she would take a rest as well, but dinner would not cook itself. Fluster wound dangerously around her feet and meowed vociferously, so she followed him into the kitchen and gave him a scoop of kibble. *I wonder what I should prepare.* She didn't feel like cooking at all. *Perhaps a short lie down is in order.*

⁓

Marge woke to the pealing of the doorbell. Hopping out of bed and running for the stairs, her socked feet slid on the carpet, and she finished her trek to the front door on her rather ample derriere. Thump, thump, thump, she bounced from one step to the next, landing at the bottom, slightly out of breath. Rising slowly, to make sure no damage had been done, she opened the front door.

Joey stood on the front porch with a concerned look on his face. "What happened? I heard thumping."

"It was nothing, but I haven't made dinner. I was feeling fatigued and inadvertently dozed."

Following her into the kitchen, Joey suggested, "We could go to the Fireside."

"I might have told Pastor Greg you were indisposed."

"Well, I was… Are you limping?"

Marge changed the subject. "I believe some leftovers are residing in the freezer. I'll confirm availability." She pulled open the freezer door, her head disappearing inside, then her arms, withdrawing with two packages and small flakes of frost on her mammoth bun. "How about ham and mashed potatoes? We can discuss our mission while they defrost."

Marge placed their dinner in the microwave to defrost and sat at the kitchen table with a pencil and paper. Joey sat and took up the pencil.

⁕⁕⁕

That evening, four adults sat around the formal table in the Beaumondes' dining room, tensely waiting for their dinner to be served. Elizabeth had unwisely presented her mother with a brochure from a new senior care center when she entered the room, although Millicent had been very clear about her thoughts on the subject.

"This is my home, and I won't be moving any time soon." She placed her napkin emphatically on her lap.

"Perhaps you should sign a Power of Attorney then," Elizabeth's husband, Reginald suggested. "Imagine what would happen if you became incapable of managing the household expenses or making your own medical decisions. Wouldn't you want us to be able to help you?"

Millicent felt heat suffusing her face. "You have a lot of nerve, Reginald. I'm seventy, not ninety, and in perfect possession of my faculties." *I need to go see that lawyer tomorrow. This is ridiculous.*

She narrowed her eyes at her son-in-law. "The milk plant has always produced plenty of income for the family to live on. Perhaps if you managed it properly and Elizabeth curbed her shopping, you wouldn't have to worry about getting your hands on the principle."

Elizabeth blushed, but Reginald continued with no sense of propriety. "See? Paranoia is one of the first signs of dementia. I think a Power of Attorney is long overdue."

"If I decide to invoke a Power of Attorney, Gavin would be the logical choice, as my first born."

Reginald's eyes widened in surprise and Elizabeth gasped. Although he bore a marked resemblance to Elizabeth, Millicent's news brought a hush to the table.

Reginald glared at Gavin and clamped his mouth shut.

Elizabeth sat stiffly in her chair and played with her napkin.

"Where are the children this evening?" Millicent asked, changing the subject. The maid arrived with the first course, and everyone studied their plates in silence. The quietude persisted through the pumpkin soup and the endive salad.

When the entrée was served, Gavin took a bite and complemented the chef. "This is possibly the best cordon bleu I have ever eaten, and the roasted vegetables are perfectly done."

"She is good, isn't she," Millicent replied distractedly. "We're lucky to have her." After dessert, she invited Gavin into the library for a glass of sherry, where they chatted amicably above the heated argument coming from the study next door.

Chapter 2

The following morning, Marge and Joey found themselves hiding in the Beaumondes' upstairs closet. *What is that smell? Lemon?* Marge sniffed carefully. Not a crack of light could be seen around the edges of the closet door, and the complete darkness was disorienting. She strained to hear the intruder, then suddenly stilled. "Joey, I don't know what has gotten into you but knock it off," she whispered irritably.

"Knock what off?"

A chill ran up Marge's spine, and she swallowed hard. "Isn't that your hand on my..."

"Marge. Don't scream. I'll turn on my phone light." Joey pointed his phone in her direction, and it shone on the body of a man propped up against the wall next to her.

She took a deep breath and started letting strings of stinkers, as she was wont to do when she was nervous. Joey pointed his phone at her face when she began to hyperventilate. "We need to get out of this closet right now," she whispered vehemently. "Whether or not we get caught."

Carefully twisting the door handle, Joey slowly stepped into the hall, and Marge knocked him right over in her haste to escape the closet. Falling together, they rolled until a pair of khaki slacks and black boots stopped their progress. Marge looked up at the strapping young man and squeaked, "Petey?"

Wide-eyed and fanning his nose, Sergeant Peter Locke gulped and stepped back. "Why were you two in the closet? Or don't I want to know?"

Marge sat up, blinking rapidly to unstick her malfunctioning fake eyelashes.

"We came to visit Millicent and observed a broken window, so we decided to investigate. We heard someone come in, probably you, so we hid."

Peter held his breath.

"It smelled funny in there, and then a hand that wasn't Joey's touched me somewhere it shouldn't have. There's someone in there who is no longer able to control their hands, Petey!"

The string of stinkers began again.

Peter backed up some more. "How can you stand it?" he mouthed to Joey as he gave him a hand up off the floor, sliding his walker, which he had left outside the closet door, within reach.

"I can hear them, but I'm nose blind." Joey chuckled and elbowed the young officer.

Peter shook his head. "Lucky you. My eyes are watering." Walking soundlessly to the closet and shining his powerful flashlight inside, he paused before glancing at his aunt. "Did you know him?"

"I didn't get a very good look." Marge joined Peter at the door and leaned in. The man in the closet had been slender, with high cheekbones, a firm jaw, straight dark hair, and hazel eyes. "I don't think I've ever seen him before, but he bears an uncanny resemblance to Elizabeth."

"He does. We got a call at the station about a break in. Did anyone see you enter the house?"

"Absolutely not! The caller wanted you to discover the body." Marge crossed her arms, her immense bun swaying dangerously.

"You said the closet smelled funny."

"Yes. Like fruit... and wood."

"I can't smell anything but... um... I have to call this in. Is there anything else you want to share? How did you get in?"

"We have our ways." Marge tried to lift an eyebrow, but it was more of a brow wiggle.

Peter sighed. "Did you break any windows or doors?"

"Nope."

"You said there was a broken window when you got here?"

"Just the one in the front. We didn't want to make a mess, so we went around back."

"Didn't it occur to you that someone else had broken in?"

Glancing at Joey, Marge said, "We were on a mission. Plus, the glass was on the outside of the house."

"Did you touch anything?"

"Yes, but we're wearing gloves, as you can see." She paused. "Where are your gloves, Joey?"

"I don't know." Removing his cowboy hat, he patted his forehead with a handkerchief. "It was hot in there."

Peter sighed again. "I'll find them. You two go home, and I'll call this in."

Marge's brow furrowed, and she pursed her lips but nodded her assent. She led Joey out the way they came in, but when they got outside, she stopped. "What about the clues?"

"Maybe Peter will find them. Let's go see what's going on at the festival." He reached out and plucked the stray eyelashes from Marge's forehead, handing them to her before heading down the hill.

<hr>

Buckwood was a very small town, population slightly over 3,500, but large enough that Marge and Joey didn't know everyone. Additionally, the Buckeye Festival drew throngs from neighboring towns and vacationers from out of state, transforming the ordinarily sleepy town into one that was crowded and full of unfamiliar energy. Cars jammed the intersections as they waited for hordes of boisterous festivalgoers to cross, and lines snaked along the sidewalks outside familiar cafes and restaurants.

Marge stinkered, walking closer to Joey's side as they slowly made their way to the green. She was relieved to hear a familiar, well-modulated voice. "Good morning Ms. Bumfuzzle, Mr. Cattywampus." Pastor Greg pushed his glasses up higher on his small nose and smiled kindly.

"Good morning, Pastor Greg. What brings you to this side of town?"

"I've been to visit a member of our flock. I trust you are feeling better, Mr. Cattywampus."

"Much better, thank you."

Marge could tell he felt guilty. Using his health to excuse their absence at Bible study the night before had been her idea since she had insisted they plan their investigation instead.

"Will you be at church on Sunday?"

"Yes, I believe so."

"Excellent! Are you on your way to see the pageant?"

"And to take a shot at the horseshoes," Joey said. "Marge has me doing yoga to improve my balance."

Greg smiled vaguely and nodded before giving them a wave, his attention diverted by another church member.

Crossing the final intersection, Marge and Joey arrived at the green, filled with patrons and activities and practically unrecognizable. They joined the jostling multitudes gathered around the temporary stage on the east side of the park.

"Do you mind if I go warm up for the horseshoe competition?" Joey asked. "I'll be back before the show."

"Okay, but you won't take your turn without me, will you? I intend to spectate."

"No, I won't."

"Go then. We have twenty minutes before the pageant begins."

She watched Joey walk away until she lost sight of him. With one side of his body slightly shorter than the other, his walker assisted him with his balance; otherwise, he was in excellent physical condition. The retractable wheels even allowed him to run when necessary or when Marge decided they needed to take up jogging.

Turning her attention to the crowd, Marge scanned the area for friends and neighbors. She was engulfed by a sea of humanity; bright clothing, gesticulating arms, and scampering children surged around her like the tide.

The din of a hundred voices, blaring radios, and barking dogs inundated her head. Marge closed her eyes and focused her ears.

"I think it's fixed. He wins every year."

"Ellie's going to win for sure!"

"Did you hear what happened at the library?"

"He'll get his. It's karma."

Her eyes flew open, and she scanned the area around her with a shiver but couldn't figure out who had said that last phrase. Everyone around her was smiling and enjoying themselves. *Maybe enjoying themselves a little too much.* She wrinkled her nose when she smelled something skunky. *I wish Joey would hurry back.*

The crowd lurched back as a dog raced through the crowd, followed by two others, dragging their leashes. *Harbingers of ill will.* Marge continued following their progress as Joey sidled up beside her, and festive music swelled through large speakers on either side of the stage. Marge grabbed his arm to steady herself, trying to see what was going on around her.

Elizabeth Beaumonde, Millicent's middle-aged daughter and president of the Ladies' Auxiliary Club, climbed the steps to the stage in mile-high stiletto heels. Marge admired her chic skirt and jacket and her sparkling jewelry. She ran her hand along her polyester pantsuit. Just looking at that beautiful suit made her skin itch.

Mrs. Beaumonde strode confidently across the stage to the microphone, suddenly breaking into a peculiar, shuffling dance. Her eyes looked like donuts as her feet flew upward, and she was propelled off the end of the stage. The crowd froze as she sailed through the air, then surged forward to see if she was okay. She was not.

Marge called Peter.

"What happened?" Joey asked, squinting.

"There's something on the stage. Let's try to get closer." They scooched through the crush toward the steps. "Keep lookout," Marge stage whispered above the noise of the crowd and the music.

She went up several steps in a crouch and couldn't believe her eyes. Reversing, she rejoined Joey. "There are buckeyes all over the stage. Dozens and dozens of them. Lend me your phone." She went back up and took some pictures.

Joey took off his cowboy hat and wiped his forehead with his handkerchief. "How'd they get there?"

"Must have been when those dogs ran through the crowd."

"What is it with the dogs this year?"

"A distraction. The saboteur is a magician, and his sleight of hand is quite accomplished." Searching around the edges of the stage, she found a mysterious, opaque bag caught in the bushes. She looked inside and found three buckeyes and some crumbs. Taking a sniff, she smelled bacon. "Look Joey, here's the bag he used. I'll keep it for Peter."

Chapter 3

In deference to Mrs. Beaumonde, the pageant was postponed, but other festival events continued as scheduled. After searching briefly for further evidence, Marge and Joey ambled across the green to the horseshoe pitch, situated on the north side, among a stand of willow trees. Marge sat on a bench beside a surly-looking teenage boy in baggy clothing who ignored her polite greeting. He scowled, shoulders hunched, strawberry-blonde hair hanging in his eyes, freckles glowing in the late-morning sun.

The rules in the Buckwood tournament were slightly unorthodox due to the number of people who entered each year. During the first few rounds, the best score between two players determined who remained. The announcer drew names out of a hat. The first contestant was old Mr. Peterson. He was close to ninety and won every year. Marge suspected that Joey's primary goal in life was to beat him.

Mr. Peterson, playing against a young man in a business suit, moved slowly to the pitch, took his aim, wobbled slightly, then threw a ringer. The small crowd roared. He then bent to pick up his second horseshoe and needed someone to help him straighten. Aiming carefully, he threw the second horseshoe. It landed five inches away from the post.

"Five points for Mr. Peterson! Next up, Oliver Drake!"

Marge hadn't met Oliver but recognized him as the new milk plant supervisor. He picked up his first horseshoe, smiled, and gave a thumbs up in Marge's direction. She looked at the boy beside her and saw him return a small thumbs up. *Must be his dad.* Oliver turned his attention back to the pitch. He threw for four points, but without a ringer, he lost to Mr. Peterson.

Over a hundred entries were whittled down to fifty, then twenty-five. Marge was glad to hear they would resume the next day because she was getting hungry.

Taking a seat beside her on the bench, Joey wore a big, lopsided grin, and his gray eyes sparkled. "I've been watching Peterson. I think I have a good chance this year."

"It's the yoga," Marge teased. "We should procure some sustenance. You must maintain your verve."

Joey stood and reached out to give her a hand up. Marge was quite slender, but for some reason, the walker prevented Joey from getting the correct leverage. First, she didn't budge, then when she pushed upwards, she knocked him over. With her colossal, red bun in his face and his arms pinned by his walker, Joey mumbled, "We're going to have to stop this, or people might get the wrong idea."

Marge lifted her head. "Speaking of which..."

Harriet McGillicutty, a moral majority of one, flounced over with her hands on her hips. "Just because you're old doesn't mean you can't be arrested for indecency."

"Could you give me a hand, Harriet? Joey's walker might have caused some permanent damage... And who are you calling old?" Marge held a hand up to Harriet, who reluctantly gave a pull. It was enough to get Marge up to her knees. "Yoga or not, I don't bounce. Are you okay, Joey?"

Joey was laughing so hard that his eyes were watering. He rolled over onto his knees, then straightened his legs. "Look. Downward dog."

Harriet gaped, her wispy, brown bob practically quivering in disapproval.

"Why didn't I think of that? Maybe we should start a yoga in the park group."

"That's all we need," Harriet exclaimed, eyes rolling and hand on her sweater-clad chest.

"Aunt Marge!"

Marge looked past Harriet and saw Peter waving.

"We must bid you adieu, Harriet. Will we see you at the dance this evening?"

"Of course! I always do my civic duty."

"See you later then." Marge and Joey headed toward Peter. "Would you like to join us for lunch, Petey? The multitudes have doubtless dwindled by this time."

"No, I'm on duty. I wanted to talk to you about what happened earlier, though."

"At the pageant?"

"Yes. You were there, right?"

Marge nodded.

"Could you come back and find me after lunch?"

Marge looked at Joey, who shrugged.

"Fine with me," he said.

"I'd like to visit Elizabeth in the hospital if she's permitted visitors."

"I'll check on that for you."

Taking their leave and continuing across the green and crossing the street to the Fireside Café, Marge opened the door and held it so Joey could get his walker through. True to its name, the café housed a flickering fire in a sizeable brick fireplace. Antique lamps glowed softly on each table, and the wooden floor and walls lent a cozy ambiance.

Sally looked up from the register and smiled when the little bell on the door tinkled. "Hello, Ms. Bumfuzzle, Mr. Cattywampus. Sit anywhere you like, and I'll be right with you." She hadn't been in town long, but Fireside regulars enjoyed her amiable disposition and ready smile.

Joey smiled back and followed Marge to a sturdy wooden table right in the center of the restaurant. Besides having the best food in town, the Fireside also had the best gossip.

They sat quietly, soaking up the atmosphere. The ebb and flow of conversation swirled around them. Marge closed her eyes and concentrated.

"Did you hear about Elizabeth Beaumonde?"

"Freida broke up with him when he got fired."

"Cut off every rose."

"She's in the hospital. They can't find Reginald."

"Why did they fire him?"

"I heard they found him leaving the Goodnight Inn with his shirt inside out."

"Not her prize roses?"

The conversations overlapped, but Marge expected Joey to help piece them together when they got home.

Sally startled her when she materialized at their table with her order pad. "What will you two be having today?"

"What's the special?" Joey asked.

"The Cuban sandwich and a bowl of tomato soup."

"I'll have that."

"Me too. It sounds exotic."

"It's very good. Can I bring you something to drink?"

"Just water, thanks."

"Coming right up."

Silence reigned when Mrs. Beaumonde senior entered the café.

"Millicent," Marge waved. "Would you like to join us?"

Although elderly and somewhat plump, Mrs. Beaumonde had excellent posture and was impeccably groomed. She walked carefully over to Marge and Joey's table, and her stern lips turned up slightly when Marge pulled out a chair for her. "It's lovely to see you, Marge. Did you, by chance, witness Elizabeth's accident this morning?"

"I did. I thought I might visit her later."

Millicent's thin eyebrows rose, and her lips pursed. "I didn't realize you two were friends."

"We aren't exactly, but she's still a member of the community."

"That's kind of you." Her shoulders relaxed slightly.

"Are you going to make something for the potluck?"

Marge paused. "Yes, I will prepare an offering."

"I'm going to make a breakfast souffle. I bought all the ingredients yesterday."

"Everyone loves your souffles. That's a wonderful choice," Joey said.

Mrs. Beaumonde was a good distraction, but Marge's stomach was getting violent by the time Sally returned. She set down the Cubans and took Millicent's order: a green salad with dressing on the side. Millicent's eyes widened when Marge and Joey opened their sandwiches and began their ritual swapping of ingredients. She watched in fascination as Marge gave Joey her bacon, and he gave her his pickles. She gave him her tomatoes, and he gave her his onions. They both took a bite.

"This is pretty good," Joey said.

"It is. You should have tried it with the pickles."

"You know I don't like them."

"I know. They do add to the sandwich, though."

Joey shrugged and took another bite.

Sally returned with Millicent's salad. "Can I get you anything else, Mrs. Beaumonde?"

"No, dear. This looks delicious." Eying her luncheon companions, Millicent placed her napkin on her lap and drizzled dressing on her salad.

Halfway through lunch, Harriet rushed into the café. "Marge! Someone shaved off Fluster's tail!"

Chapter 4

Everyone in the café began speaking at once except Marge, who was stunned. She stood and stared at Harriet. "Where is he?"

"He's hiding under the stage."

Marge walked out the door as if in a trance, then she started to run. She ran to the stage, then dropped to her knees, round, lavender-clad bottom in the air. It was dark under the stage, but she could see two glowing eyes. "Fluster? Come to mommy. It's okay." The eyes blinked, but Fluster didn't move. "Come on, baby. I'll take you home." Marge was offered a blanket, and she knew Joey was there with her. Her eyes started to sting with unshed tears. He was always there for her. "Come on, Fluster. Look, I have a nice blanket for you."

"Everyone back up, please," Joey said. "Let's make Fluster feel safe."

After about fifteen minutes, Fluster finally approached Marge, who wrapped him up and carried him home. Joey called Dr. Harkins on the way and asked if he could make a house call. Peter called Marge's phone, and Joey explained what happened, so by the time they arrived at Marge's house, Dr. Harkins and Peter were deep in conversation on the front porch.

They all entered Marge's busy living room and sat down. Marge passed Fluster to the vet, and surprisingly, he went without complaint. He and the doc didn't have a friendly relationship, although Dr. Harkins was, in fact, an excellent veterinarian. He was gentle and loved all his patients. Lightly stroking Fluster and speaking to him in a soothing voice while visually inspecting the tail, everything went well until he touched it to look underneath.

Fluster meowed angrily and swiped at him with his claws extended. Dr. Harkins flinched but stayed quiet as blood dripped from his hand.

Joey unobtrusively fetched a roll of paper towels.

Having made his point, Fluster jumped off the vet's lap and rubbed against Marge's shin before heading toward his food bowl in the kitchen.

"Is he okay?" Marge asked anxiously.

"Physically, yes, although he is rightly upset about his tail. Someone must have held him down and used an electric shaver."

"How did they get a hold of him? He is very particular about who he gets close to," Joey said.

"That I don't know."

"Who would do something like this?" Marge stared into space. "Will it grow back?"

"It should grow back, but it might not be quite the same."

Peter said, "The who and why are the reason I'm here. We need to talk about what's happening around town."

"On that note," Dr. Harkins stood, "I'll take my leave. If you notice any signs of malaise or unusual behavior, give me a call."

"Thank you, doctor. It was exceedingly kind of you to come."

"I know how much you love that boy of yours. I'm glad there wasn't any serious harm done."

Joey showed him out, then returned to the living room.

"We have several things happening, and I don't know if they're connected," Peter said.

"The body in the closet," said Joey.

"Yes, and the disruptions at the festival," Marge added.

"Right." Peter nodded. "Now we seem to have vandals around town: graffiti on the library, Mrs. Essex's roses, Fluster's tail, and Mayor Wright's tires."

The three of them sat in silence for a moment. Marge stinkered a couple of times.

"What did you mean this morning when you said you were looking for clues?" Peter looked at Marge.

"Yesterday, after the canine debacle, Reginald smelled like bacon."

"Marge thought we might find some clues pointing to his involvement."

"And did you?"

"I don't know." Marge fluffed her curly, red hair. "We found someone who crossed over to the other side."

"I went through the medicine cabinets and found a prescription for an MAOI. Do you know anything about those?"

"I know they are utilized in treating depression, and certain types have stringent dietary restrictions. Did you discover the source of the unusual smell in the closet?"

"No, not yet. Were you present when Mrs. Beaumonde had her accident?"

"That was not an accident."

"How do you know?"

"The harbinger and the bag."

Peter stared at his aunt and ran a sturdy hand through his wavy, auburn hair.

"You know how the dogs wrecked the judging tables?" Joey asked.

Peter nodded.

"Well, several dogs, trailing leashes, ran through the audience before the pageant began. Marge thinks they were a distraction so someone could scatter the buckeyes without anyone noticing."

"And you found the bag they were in?"

"Marge found it."

"How does she know that's the bag they were in?"

"I know because it still contained a few buckeyes. Also, I am sitting right here. Why are you talking like I'm not here? You can see me, right?" She looked at her hand as if it might be invisible.

"Of course, we can see you." Joey leaned forward. "Sorry about that. I was just trying to help."

"I photographed the stage lest someone elected to eradicate the evidence before you examined it."

"May I see the photos?"

Marge nodded to Joey, who handed Peter his phone.

"It *was* cleaned off. Good thinking, Aunt Marge. I must get back to the station. Could you forward those pictures to my phone?" Peter stood.

"What about the vandalism? You mentioned that too."

"You've been a big help, but stay out of this now, okay?"

Marge and Joey gazed at him, looking as innocent as a couple of puppies.

Chapter 5

After stopping at the station to print the pictures Joey had sent him and tacking them on the board, Peter decided to interview the Beaumondes. Their generous donations to the police and fire fund meant that the captain considered them beyond reproach, but the body was found in their hall closet. Braving his captain's wrath, Peter headed for the big house on the hill. He parked in the circular drive, which framed a Grecian-looking fountain, and approached the front door with apprehension.

His knock was answered by a young maid wearing a modest black dress and a white apron. The house, which could be labelled a mansion, currently accommodated three generations of five Beaumondes. Although Elizabeth was in the hospital, her husband and mother were home, and the maid left Peter in the large foyer while she went to find Reginald. Peter glanced nervously at the enormous chandelier hanging from the high ceiling above his head, then let his eyes glide by two hallways and five closed doors, up the wide, curving staircase, to the ornate railing above.

Reginald strode in and greeted him with a flourish, startling him. "I'm on my way to the milk plant, but I have a moment if you'll join me in the study. Daisy is bringing a coffee tray." Peter followed him down the hallway on the left to one of the closed doors, thinking of the game *Clue* and wondering how many rooms were used on a daily basis.

Seating himself in a comfortable leather chair, Reginald indicated that Peter should sit in its twin, across from him. Daisy, the maid who had answered the door, brought the coffee tray and poured them each a cup before silently leaving the room.

Reginald glanced at his watch and took a sip of coffee. "What can I do for you, Sergeant?"

"As you may know, Mr. Beaumonde, we have been experiencing a crime wave of sorts this weekend, and since you have been involved in some of the incidents, directly or indirectly, I'd like to ask you a few questions."

Reginald raised a well-sculpted brow, looking slightly amused. "Does your captain know you're here?"

"No, but I don't believe we can have a proper investigation if we exclude anyone. Imagine if CSI aired a murder investigation that occurred inside someone's house and didn't interview the residents. They would lose all credibility."

"So, we must follow proper procedure." Reginald nodded importantly, taking another sip. "Where shall we begin?"

Flipping open his notebook, Peter said, "Let's begin with the victim found in the upstairs closet. Did you know him?"

"No, I had never met him before."

"Do you know why he was in your home?"

"Mother said he was a relative, so I suppose he had come to visit her."

"Weren't you curious about why he was here?"

"I was busy and didn't actually meet him, but I knew Elizabeth would unravel the mystery and tell me all about it at the most inconvenient time possible."

"Could you tell me your whereabouts on Thursday and Friday mornings, between seven and nine?"

Reginald canted his head and tapped his thin lips with a manicured index finger. "I usually wake at six and go to the milk plant, but on Thursday, I left the plant around nine to see how the festival preparation was going."

"Do you recall what you had for breakfast?"

Reginald laughed. "Breakfast? No. I usually eat whatever has been prepared or grab a piece of toast."

"Do you ever cook anything for yourself? Bacon, for example?"

"Very rarely. My culinary skills are quite lacking."

"And Friday morning?"

"That was the morning of the murder, wasn't it? I went to the plant as usual and let everyone leave at lunch time so they could enjoy the festival. We'll close early again today for the same reason."

"Sounds like you are a very considerate boss. I hope your employees appreciate you."

"Most of them do, I think. They're a good bunch."

"Have you had any trouble at the factory?"

"Not really, just the one employee who was caught stealing."

"One final question. Have you had any trouble with vandalism lately? We've had multiple reports this week."

"No. I've heard some rumors but haven't experienced any myself. Knock on wood." Reginald smiled wryly.

Peter nodded and stood, extending his hand to shake Reginald's. "Thank you very much for your cooperation, Mr. Beaumonde. Do you suppose you could send your mother-in-law in to speak with me?"

"I believe she's in the kitchen. I'll show you the way, then I must get back to the plant." Peter followed him back into the hall and behind the staircase to a large open kitchen filled with gleaming appliances and a large, old-fashioned wooden table. "Mother, there is a policeman to see you," he announced before unceremoniously leaving the room.

Millicent turned with a smile. "Hello, Peter. Would you like some fresh-baked cookies?"

"Yes, ma'am. Your cookies are the best in the county."

Placing three cookies on a small plate with a spatula and pouring a small glass of milk, she delivered both to the kitchen table and took a seat. "Please sit down and tell me what I can do for you."

Peter sat and took a bite of his cookie, smiling happily before launching into his spiel. He liked Mrs. Beaumonde senior considerably more than her daughter and son-in-law.

Once he explained the purpose of his visit, Millicent's cheeks turned pink, and she looked down at her wedding ring.

It glistened in the sunlight streaming through the window as she twisted it around her finger. "When I was a young woman, newly married, my husband went off to war and left me all alone in this big house. I was lonely and made friends with a handsome young man who delivered groceries. The result was a son I couldn't claim, and my midwife helped me place him for adoption. I didn't know who adopted him or what his name was, but when he showed up a few days ago, I knew it was him; he looked just like Elizabeth." She stood and brought more cookies to the table.

"What did Elizabeth and Reginald think of your visitor?"

She shrugged. "I introduced him by name and didn't tell them who he was, but they aren't stupid. I'm sure they could put two and two together. He was very polite and circumspect, speaking with me privately about my past and his adoption. I would have enjoyed getting to know him better." She frowned, and her eyes drooped. "Funny thing is that he knew Sally Drake before he came here. I don't know how they met; he was quite a bit older, but she brought over a cake after he arrived."

"Do you have any thoughts about who might have killed him?"

"I guess it couldn't have been an accident since he was in the closet."

"Unlikely."

"Elizabeth and Reginald are overtly interested in their inheritance, but I can't imagine them killing a family member over it. Perhaps it was someone from his past who followed him here." She picked up a cookie and took a bite.

Peter looked at her kindly. "Could you tell me about Thursday and Friday mornings?"

"Well, when I came downstairs on Thursday, there was a giant breakfast prepared. I ate with Gavin, my son, and commented that it was unusual."

"Did he mention any food allergies or dietary restrictions?"

"No, he seemed to eat everything."

"And Friday?"

"I came downstairs, and there was no breakfast and no Gavin. I must admit I was a little disappointed but figured I would see him at dinner. I was shocked to discover police cars when I returned."

"Who is in charge of breakfast?"

Millicent looked at Peter and blinked. "In charge? No one at the moment. The cook no longer makes breakfast because everyone leaves at different times and has their own dietary preferences. Reginald leaves at six, Elizabeth usually gets up at seven or eight and won't eat anything she thinks might be fattening, and the children leave at eight and want donuts or muffins."

"So, who made breakfast on Thursday?"

"I don't know." She tilted her head like a little bird. "Isn't that strange? I wonder if Gavin made it. It sure was delicious."

"Thank you very much for the interview and the cookies." Peter stood. "You're my favorite witness." He smiled and winked at her.

Millicent's cheeks turned pink, and she smiled as she walked him out. "Stop by any time, Peter. It was a lovely visit."

Chapter 6

Once Peter left, Marge hurried over to her desk and pulled out a notepad and a pencil. "Let's review each incident and determine if any of the victims or occurrences could be related. Who are the victims?"

Joey thought about that and ticked them off on his fingers. "The man in the closet, everyone with entries at the festival, Elizabeth Beaumonde, Mary Lou Essex, Mayor Wright, Fluster (or you), and the library (or Roger Mathison)."

Marge tapped her pencil on the notebook. "We'll add in some of the conversations we overheard at the café."

"I'm afraid I wasn't paying much attention."

"Well, people were talking about Elizabeth's accident and Mrs. Essex's roses. Several mentioned someone who was released from duty."

"That must have been James Nelson. Reginald accused him of stealing."

Marge nodded. "Someone said Freida broke up with him. Then there was discussion about someone seen leaving a motel. Who would that be?"

"Probably Reginald. He has quite the reputation."

"His indiscretions and firing James could be motives."

"Motives for what? There's a lot going on."

Marge shrugged. "Four events are connected to the Beaumondes, four could be connected to our Bible study group, two to the city, and three to the festival. We need more information."

"They might not all be connected."

Marge stared at him.

"Murder and vandalism are not the same type of crime."

"True. Should we return to the festival? Perhaps we could call on Elizabeth first."

"Why are you so concerned with visiting her?"

"I'm not sure. Something irregular is transpiring. The bacon, the man in the closet, the gossip about Reginald, Elizabeth's accident… too many coincidences. Are you about ready to go?"

"Yes. Do you want to change first?" He pointed at the grass stains on her purple polyester trousers.

"I probably should. Could you feed Fluster for me?"

"Sure. Come on, you poor, malnourished beast."

Fluster followed Joey into the bright, yellow kitchen with his skinny tail in the air. He was obviously not underfed, but with his long, fluffy hair removed, he wasn't as large as he looked, either. "You must be half fur, at least." Joey poured a scoop of food in his bowl and watched him devour every bite.

"Okay, I'm ready," Marge called.

Joey left the kitchen, rounded the corner, and blinked. Marge was wearing the brightest trousers he'd ever seen. Large pink, orange, and purple triangles covered her from her waist to her bell bottoms.

"Do you like them?" She smiled and twirled. "I hear bell bottoms are back in style, and this way, I don't have to change my blouse. These trousers match everything."

"Very festive, Marge." He smiled at her enthusiasm as he opened the door.

Marge followed him across the street and waited as he backed his lovingly restored 1929 Ford Model A out of his garage and closed the door.

Climbing into the passenger seat, she said, "I feel like a celebrity when we take your car. Everyone smiles and waves."

"I must admit I'm a little nervous about taking her out right now. Hopefully, we'll be out of the vandals' sights."

"They have hitherto focused on the vicinity in close proximity to the green."

Keeping his hands at ten and two, Joey nodded but concentrated on the road.

The hospital was a mere five minutes by car, and they pulled into the parking spot closest to the front entrance. Joey locked the doors and set the alarm before they walked through double sets of glass doors and into a lobby oddly reminiscent of a garden gazebo. The usual library-level quiet had been transformed into chaotic cacophony as the lobby filled with injured festivalgoers. When their turn came to approach the front desk, the harried receptionist handed them a packet of papers and asked after their complaints. "We're here to visit a patient," Marge explained. "Could you tell us where we can find Elizabeth Beaumonde?"

"Ordinarily, I would take you there, but we are swamped. She's in room 320. Take that elevator to the third floor and turn left."

"Thank you very much. I hope the onslaught abates soon."

The receptionist's directions were easy to follow, and once they had boarded the elevator, the noise-level dropped considerably.

Marge tapped on the door to room 320 and received a musical come in, so she pushed the door open and stepped inside. Elizabeth's eyes went wide, and she blinked as her right hand went to her neck. Marge smiled at her ambiguous greeting. "Joey and I witnessed your accident this afternoon, and we just wanted to let you know we're thinking of you and hope you get well soon."

"You shouldn't have," she choked.

"What is that exquisite perfume you're wearing?"

"It's Tiziana Terenzi Cubia and $570 a bottle, so you probably can't afford it."

"Yes, very exclusive. A bouquet of lemons… and some kind of wood… cedar or sandalwood?"

"If you look it up, you can find all of the ingredients." Elizabeth pursed her lips.

Studying Elizabeth's oval face and high cheekbones, Marge was reminded of the man in the closet. *It's an ignominy, all that beauty marred by such an uncharitable disposition.*

"Do you require provisions?" Marge looked around and saw that someone had brought the comforts of home. "Any necessities we could convey? Some festival food perhaps?"

Elizabeth's lip curled up. "No, thank you. So kind. I think I should rest now."

Marge smiled again. "Please advise us if you find yourself lacking. We're at your disposal."

She and Joey left the room and returned to the car. "Did you notice her perfume?"

"You know I'm nose blind."

"That's what I smelled in the closet this morning. Her bracelet is very unusual. It reminds me of the Garden of Eden. Do people usually wear jewelry in the hospital?"

"She was wearing makeup and a fancy nightgown too. I wonder who she's expecting."

Marge shrugged and waited for Joey to unlock her car door.

When they pulled into his driveway, she decided to go back inside and retrieve her sweater. "The sun is setting, and the air is cool. You might also welcome the extra warmth."

Nodding, Joey assured her he would bring his sweater, then carefully maneuvered his car into the garage. They met back outside and began their walk to the town green.

Marge, and therefore Joey, considered their evening walk an excellent opportunity for exercise, and they inevitably ran into friends and neighbors, who shared local news and their varied opinions about said news. That evening was no exception. Mrs. Waddle, in a pink housecoat and matching slippers, was out walking her dog and stopped to commiserate with Marge about Fluster's tail. "Poor thing. I'm afraid to even let Sir Chewalot out in the yard anymore."

"Completely understandable," Marge said. "Fluster was quite traumatized."

"I believe it. I hope they catch the scoundrels soon."

"You think it's more than one person?"

"Oh, yes." Mrs. Waddle nodded vigorously. "One of those gangs of kids, I imagine."

"Will you be attending the dance this evening?"

"No, I don't think so. Dancing is for the youngsters."

"We're headed there now, so look for us if you change your mind."

"Of course. You two, be careful. Who knows when that gang will strike again."

They made it to the next block before Mr. Flannigan stopped them outside his butcher shop. Marge had to refrain from calling him Mr. Cardigan. He pulled his high-waisted pants toward his chest and straightened his ever-present sweater. "Hello, Joey. When will you be joining us for cards again?"

"When will you be playing next?" Joey countered.

"After the festival. I must keep an eye on the shop right now, with those vandals about."

Joey nodded empathetically. "Have they damaged any of the shops?"

"No, just the library so far and Mrs. Essex's roses. I don't want to take any chances, though."

"No, of course not. Let me know when you arrange a game. We must move along."

On an ordinary evening, Marge and Joey were stopped several times, but the townsfolk were garrulous on the subject of the recent spate of vandalism.

Sitting at a small wrought iron table outside the I Spy Ice Cream shop, Roger Mathison, the town librarian, waved enthusiastically. Sharing his table was none other than Harriet McGillicutty, wearing a starched cotton dress and matching turquoise sweater. "What do you think about the vandalism, Marge?" Roger's fingers trembled slightly as he ran them through his bushy, brown mustache.

"Why are you asking her?" Harriet sounded annoyed. "She's just an old nosy parker."

"She usually knows what's going on, that's why."

Joey's head followed the conversation like a ping-pong spectator.

"It's curious. We have a plethora of misconduct coinciding with a revered and beloved town event. What do you suppose? Any inkling about this surfeit of enmity?" Marge asked.

Roger shook his head, his eyebrows pointing downward in a V-shape.

"Why don't you talk like a normal person? I think it's that little troublemaker, Carter Beaumonde, and his pack of hooligans." Harriet crossed her arms over her ample chest.

"Did you observe them in the vicinity of the stage when you found Fluster?" Marge asked.

"I didn't notice them, but there were kids running around everywhere."

"We'll keep our eyes open," Joey said.

Chapter 7

The green came into sight, and Marge's stomach growled. "We were unable to complete lunch."

"Are you interested in sampling the festival food?"

"Let's take an inventory of the offerings." She shivered. "I'm grateful for my sweater.

"The dancing should heat us up, and we can always get a drink at the Fireside if we need to." Joey winked.

The town green was bursting with life. The lights on the rides and the arcade glowed as the sun began to set, transforming the park into a magical land of entertainment. Families with children and dogs, couples and teenagers with their own agendas, milled around, shouting to be heard over the vociferous crowd and thunderous music. Despite the frenetic sound and activity, no festival would be complete without the delightful aromas of popcorn, cotton candy, and barbecue. Joey and Marge wandered around, pondering the food trucks and their long lines, discussing their culinary options.

"Gyros are Greek food, are they not?"

"Yes. Lamb, I think."

"That sounds exotic. Should we sample them?"

All the tables were occupied, and as Joey watched people trying to eat their gyros, he thought they looked messy. "Do you think we could dance a little until some of the tables are free?"

"An excellent suggestion. I am disinclined to dine on my feet. Dribbling can be problematic."

The band began with a rousing square dance, which was one of Joey's favorites, and Marge helped him up the steps to the stage.

He swung her around, using the retractable wheels on his walker, and by the end of the first song, they were both panting.

"Again, again!" Marge said. "That was so fun."

Joey smiled and held out his hand, and before they knew it, they were surrounded by dozens of couples.

Harriet spun by with Roger. On their way back, she said, "Carter's gang is over by the arcade." She pointed.

<hr />

Flushed and happy, Marge said, "Let's locate provisions. I'm feeling a distinct lack of sustenance."

"Me too. Dancing works up quite an appetite."

"Aw. The gyros stand closed. Now what?"

"We could share a corndog, then have a proper dinner at the Fireside after the dance."

Marge smiled. "We can replenish our reserves and satisfy Harriet's curiosity."

They decided on two corndogs because they were small, then wandered toward the arcade, which was dark and boarded up for the night. Chewing rather than conversing, they happened upon the group of boys sitting in a circle behind one of the booths.

Marge recognized Carter and the surly-looking boy from the horseshoe pits. She stopped and put a finger to her lips. Standing in the shadows, they ate their corndogs in silence.

"I don't want to," the surly boy said.

"You'll do it, or I'll tell my dad that your dad is stealing. He'll get fired just like James did."

"Did he threaten you, too?" He looked at the other three boys.

Two of them nodded. The third said, "Quit being such a baby, Seth. If you want to be part of the group, you have to do what Carter says."

Seth hunched over and frowned.

Carter smirked, reminding Marge of his father. "All you have to do is collect a bunch of buckeyes. My dad told me what to do with them."

"Why would he want to make a bunch of old people sick?"

"He doesn't. He just wants to make a statement."

The boys got up and reluctantly began to search for nuts, so Joey and Marge moved farther away and stood close together like they were being romantic.

Carter scoffed when he saw them. "Go get a room." He tried to push Joey's walker over, but Joey's muscular hand clamped around his forearm like a vice.

"Don't start a fight you can't win, young man."

Carter's eyes widened, and he backed up, trying to play it off. Joey let him go but glared at him as he backed away, spouting scurrilous nonsense as he went. Marge noticed the boy they called Seth was watching their interaction with interest.

Once the boys had moved away from them, Joey threw away the corndog wrappers and accompanied Marge back to the dance. The music had changed from country to pop, but they didn't mind. Marge's bun bounced precariously as she studied the youngsters and tried to replicate their moves. Joey danced to his own drum, a serene smile on his face.

After the dance, they strolled to the Fireside Café, which was open late in honor of the festival. Sally had finished her shift and had been replaced by Curtis, the owner. He and Joey looked at each other with eyebrows raised when Marge chose a booth in the corner farthest from the door.

"I'm a little tired." She picked up the menu.

Joey asked Curtis if there was something on the menu they could share. Thinking that over, he suggested the appetizer platter. Marge nodded. "And a whiskey neat."

"Me too." Curtis left, and Joey looked at Marge with concern. "Penny for your thoughts."

"Mostly, I'm fatigued, but I was contemplating those boys. We must discover a means of liberating the surly youth from Carter's coercion. And perhaps we ought to recommence our karate classes."

"I thought you hated karate."

"Well, I did, but it could prove expedient. I'm not as strong as you."

"What about a different kind of martial art if you don't like karate? Like kung fu? Or jiu-jitsu?"

"I wonder if we can locate a class."

"I'll look. If not, we can always take one online."

Curtis brought their drinks and the platter. "Can I get you anything else?"

They looked at each other, shook their heads, and then picked at the food on the platter while sipping their drinks.

"I wonder where Petey's been all evening."

Joey frowned. "I wonder what those boys are planning to do with the buckeyes."

The bell on the front door tinkled, and Peter walked in.

"Sorry, we're closed," Curtis called.

"I'm just looking for my aunt. I won't order anything."

Peter joined Joey and Marge and snatched a mozzarella stick from their platter. "Learn anything new this evening?"

Marge raised her eyebrows, remembering he told them to stay out of his investigation. "We did. The unusual smell in the closet was Elizabeth's perfume."

"I went to interview her this evening. It made me sneeze."

"It's pretty potent. What did she have to say?"

"She said she didn't see why she needed to be interrogated like a common criminal, so I gave her my CSI speech, and she gave me her landed gentry look in return. 'Life is slightly different than television,' she said." Peter got a faraway look in his eyes as he thought back to their interview.

"Petey?"

Peter jerked upright. "Sorry, Aunt Marge. I was thinking about the interview. It was very uncomfortable, and I didn't learn much. She suggested the victim was a thief who had wandered into the house, and he probably stole her perfume."

"Why was it uncomfortable?"

Peter blushed. "You'll think it's ridiculous, but I got the feeling she was making a pass at me."

"Not that ridiculous. You're a very attractive young man."

"But she's…"

"Whatever she is, don't let that deter you from focusing on the case. Did you discover anything else?"

"The medical examiner found the MAOI along with a large quantity of alcohol in the victim's stomach."

"Was that what caused him to leave this earthly plain?"

"Possibly, and he didn't die in the closet."

Joey paused, a chicken wing hovering near his mouth. "Good to have that confirmed. If he *had* died in the closet, we would have to ask ourselves why." He glanced at Marge, who had been unusually quiet, then added, "We found out that Carter Beaumonde is bullying some of the local boys into helping him with the vandalism," Joey said.

"I wondered about him," Peter said.

"We should let Curtis close. Are you ready to go?" Joey asked Marge.

"Yes. Would you like a doggy bag, Petey?"

"No, I'd better not eat this late. Thanks for sharing." He looked around the café. "Where's Sally?"

"She got off at seven," Curtis said, wiping nearby tables.

"We'll head home and let you finish, Curtis. Thank you for the repast."

"It's been good to see you, Ms. Bumfuzzle. Goodnight, Mr. Cattywampus, Peter."

"Thanks for the update. I'm off duty now, so I'll head home." Peter gave them a little wave.

Strolling leisurely toward home, Joey stopped at Mrs. Essex's picket fence. Her garden, usually full of blooming roses, was conspicuously bare. Joey examined several of the branches near the fence. "The roses were cut off by someone left-handed. Look at the angle of the cuts."

Marge bent to inspect them and mimed cutting the branches with her right hand and then her left. "I believe you are correct. We should apprise Peter. Are we acquainted with anyone of the left-handed persuasion?"

"I never noticed."

"Are we still up for yoga in the morning?" Marge asked.

"Of course. I look forward to it. I have been surprised at how much it loosens me up and improves my day."

"It benefits me, too. Nine o'clock?"

"Sounds good."

They said goodnight and headed to their individual homes.

Chapter 8

The next morning, Joey was waiting for Marge when she logged onto Facetime. He had worn pajamas when they started yoga but gradually upgraded to narrow sweatpants and a tucked-in t-shirt. He tried extremely hard to not be surprised by Marge's choice of outfits, but he inevitably was. They ranged from 80s-style leotards and leg warmers to today's black tights with a purple thong and sequined bikini top. He never knew what to expect. When Pastor Greg had introduced them, Joey had anticipated quiet, recliner company, but Marge was always unpredictable. She kept him young with her flagrant disregard for others' assumptions and the way she embraced life with an effervescent sense of adventure. If not for her, he would have wallowed in his war-time trauma and given up on life.

"Are you ready for our downward dog?" she asked cheerfully. "That was a brilliant example of how yoga can be useful, by the way. Bravo."

"I'm ready if you are."

Marge put on their DVD, and they grunted and groaned through their daily regime. The sound effects were part of the fun and had become something of a competition between the two. When it was over, Marge collapsed on the ground and turned her face toward the screen. "You are much better at this than I am. Do you want to progress to DVD number two?"

"Nope. We can stay on number one forever if you ask me. Number two is just going to make us work harder."

"I'll try to improve. It's disadvantageous to remain perpetually at the same level. We should be progressing.

Shower up, and I'll meet you for breakfast in half an hour."

"Over and out."

Marge got up and walked to the bathroom. She knew Joey humored her on a regular basis, and she adored him for it. She showered and dressed in one of her favorite outfits, a lime-green pantsuit with bright pink flowers. Skipping downstairs, she fed Fluster and started breakfast, and by the time Joey knocked on her door and let himself in, she was setting their plates on the table.

"Breakfast looks delicious. What's on the agenda today?"

"Your tournament, of course, and solving mysteries."

"I'd like to find James and ask him about what happened at the factory. I know he's not a thief."

Marge placed Joey's plate on the table when he sat. She made sausage and egg on English muffins, fruit salad, and cottage cheese.

Next, she set two cups of coffee on the table and returned with her plate.

"This is one of my favorite breakfasts," Joey said between bites.

"I'm not sure there's a breakfast I don't like, except cereal, perhaps." She wrinkled her nose. "Cereal is more of a snack food."

"Did you make extra?"

"I did, but I wanted you to eat your fruit first. Would you like some more coffee?"

"Yes, please." He held out his plate and then his cup for refills.

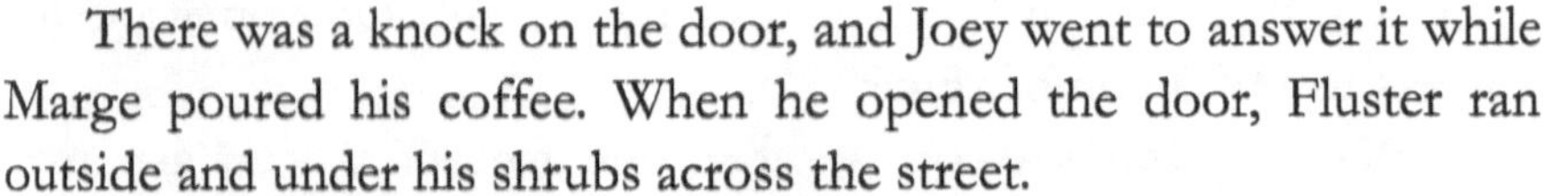

There was a knock on the door, and Joey went to answer it while Marge poured his coffee. When he opened the door, Fluster ran outside and under his shrubs across the street.

James Nelson, a large young man of twenty-eight and recently unemployed, stood on the porch, his thick, blonde hair rumpled like it hadn't seen a comb for a while, his clothes wrinkled. "Mr. Cattywampus, what have you done to your shrubs?"

Joey squinted across the street and gawked.His shrubbery, normally aligned with his house, had been cut at an angle that didn't match. "Marge. Come look at this."

Marge came to the door and looked across the street. "What on earth?"

"Come on in, James. I need to call Petey." She left the two of them to talk while she called her nephew.

When Peter arrived, Fluster ran back into the house, carrying something shiny in his mouth, and crawled under the sofa. "Hi, Aunt Marge."

"Hi, Petey. Did you see Joey's shrubs?"

He turned to look at them. Joey's house sloped diagonally downhill, and his shrubs had been cut to match the angle of the house, but someone had re-trimmed them at right angles, so they didn't match the house or the sidewalk. The average person might think they looked fine. To Joey, whose outlook was always slightly skewed, the shrubs had been defaced. Because Joey's body was slightly shorter on the right side, and his head tilted in that direction, his slanted house on his slanted street, with his diagonal bushes, looked perfectly normal to him. Whoever had trimmed his bushes in a straight line had made them look crooked. Peter, who understood, felt great outrage on Joey's behalf.

He joined Joey and James on Marge's vintage floral chintz sofa and loveseat. As usual, the patterned furniture, combined with matching draperies, busy area rugs, and a plethora of figurines, made Peter's head spin. He found it difficult to absorb all the colors and patterns without experiencing sensory overload. "Could we sit in the kitchen, Aunt Marge?"

"Certainly. Perhaps you'd all like some coffee."
The three men trooped after her into the sunny, yellow kitchen and sat at the white, rectangular table while Marge placed Joey's uneaten

breakfast sandwich in a baggie, cleared the breakfast dishes,and poured coffee. Although bright, Peter found the solid colors in the kitchen much easier to tolerate. He pulled out his notebook and pen and accepted a cup of coffee. "What time did you come over here, Joey?"

"About ten."

"The shrubbery was as usual?"

"I would like to say yes, but I wasn't really looking at it, certainly not from this side of the street."

"When was the last time you noticed it?"

"It was undamaged last night." Marge set down a plate of snickerdoodle cookies.

"And what time did you arrive, James?"

"I think it was about ten-thirty."

"I'll crawl around under the shrubs and see if I can find any clues, but the vandals have been choosing broad times when most people are asleep, so alibis are hard to come by."

"Explicate last night's discovery, Joey."

"Oh. Yes. I forgot about that. When Marge and I were walking home last night, I inspected Mrs. Essex's rosebushes and noticed the branches were cut by someone left-handed. I don't know if that will be relevant at some point, but it's worth noting."

"That should be very helpful. Thank you." He took a sip of coffee and squinted at James. "How do you know Joey?"

"I don't remember how we met, but we play Scrabble together, and sometimes I help him with his lawn."

"I remember." Joey smiled. "We were both practicing at the horseshoe pits a couple of years ago and got talking about history."

"Yes." James smiled too. "That was a great afternoon."

"I've heard rumors about you," Peter said, "but I haven't seen an official report at the station."

"That's because the only theft at the milk plant is Reginald's skimming."

Peter's eyebrows rose almost to his hairline.

"I noticed something fishy and reported it, then the next thing I knew, I was being called a thief and escorted from the building."

"Those are some serious allegations."

"Yeah, and I can't prove any of it. He has put an end to my career."

"Since he didn't file a police report, it's not official."

"Please don't point that out to him."

"We should have a private chat sometime. I would like to hear how he's going about stealing from himself."

"Sure. I have a lot of free time right now." James slumped in his chair.

Peter finished his coffee and rose to leave. "I don't know if we'll ever discover who shaved Fluster and defaced your shrubs, but each detail gets us closer, and if we do catch the vandals, any evidence we have will help us prosecute. I'll keep you informed."

"Thank you, Peter." Joey shook his hand, and Marge walked him to the front door.

Chapter 9

James and Joey remained at the kitchen table while Marge tidied upstairs. They were silent for a moment, then James set his mug on the table and leaned forward on his elbows. "I need your help."

Joey raised an eyebrow and waited.

"You know how I was fired from the milk plant?"

"Yes, but I don't believe you're a thief."

"I'm not. I noticed a discrepancy between the orders we were filling and what was being entered in the books, so I reported it to Oliver Drake, the supervisor. The next thing I knew, Mr. Beaumonde was calling me a thief. He lied to my face and ruined my career as a teamster."

"Why would he do that?"

"Like I told Peter, I'm pretty sure he's skimming from the profits."

Joey's brow furrowed.

"Anyway, the day after I was fired, I saw Mr. Beaumonde leaving the Goodnight Inn with a young woman. His shirt was on inside out, and the buttons were skewed. He walked her to her car and leaned her against it to kiss her, then walked toward his own car. Everyone knows he's having an affair with Oliver Drake's wife, and something inside me snapped. I walked toward him with a smile and told him that if he wanted me to keep his nasty little secrets, I wanted my job back."

Joey gaped at him.

"I know I shouldn't have done that. I wasn't thinking straight. But he set up a meeting with me at the milk plant tonight, at one in the morning, and I'm scared.

I'd like you to be there as backup and to witness whatever he says. Will you help me?"

Joey blew air out of pursed lips and studied James's face. "You know that was very foolish, right? And illegal? You won't ever try that again?"

"I won't. I promise. But he has scheduled the meeting, and I'm afraid to go alone. Please?"

"I'll go because you're my friend, and I don't want you to get hurt, but I don't approve of what you've done. What time do you want me there?"

"About twelve-fifty? You can use this badge to get in the employee entrance, and I'll make sure the cameras are turned off." He handed Joey a badge with a cow on it. "Thank you, Joey. I really appreciate your help."

Joey shook his hand and saw him to the door.

Once James had taken his leave, Marge reentered the kitchen and sat with Joey, who had a pensive look on his face.

"What did James wish to discuss?"

"He has landed himself in a pickle. It's not good, but I told him I'd help."

"If you're in, I'm in. Tell me."

Joey told her James's story and his request for backup.

"What time? Will we have to miss Bible study again?"

"I think so. You don't have to come if you don't want to."

"Of course, I'm coming, but Harriet is going to have a field day. You did mention to James that extortion is undesirable. And dangerous."

"I did, but it has already been set in motion."

Marge looked at him thoughtfully, then got up and poured them each one more cup of coffee. After she sat down, she opened her mouth to say something, then closed it again, taking a sip of coffee instead. Joey was about to ask her what was on her mind when she changed the subject.

"Are you prepared to defeat old man Peterson at horseshoes?"

"I believe I am. Also, the chili cookoff is this afternoon. I can't wait to try them all."

Marge nodded but wrinkled her brow. *I hope everyone cooked their beans well this year. Last year was a little embarrassing.*

As they were preparing to leave, they were interrupted by a hesitant knock.

Joey opened the door to find the surly boy from the festival standing on the stoop, fist raised to knock again. "Hello, young man. How can I help you? We were about to leave for the festival."

"I need to talk to someone about the chili cookoff." He shuffled nervously and studied his shoes.

"Come on in and sit down. What's your name?"

"Seth, sir."

Joey turned toward the kitchen. "Marge! We have company."

She came out holding Fluster, who took one look at Seth and howled before bolting upstairs. Marge squinted at the boy. "Did you participate in the disfigurement of my feline?"

He stood suddenly. "I made a mistake. I have to go."

"Sit down, please," Joey said. "The lady asked you a question."

He gulped. "I didn't do it, but I was there."

"Who was the perpetrator?" she asked very quietly.

"Randy held him down, and Carter shaved his tail. If they find out I told you, they'll beat me up and make trouble for my dad."

"We heard Carter threaten you last night. What brings you here?"

Seth squirmed in his chair. "I didn't like what they did to the cat, and I'm worried about the buckeyes."

"What are they planning to do with them?"

"Carter said his dad is planning to grind them up and put them in the chili. Raw buckeyes are poisonous, right?" He scrunched up his nose. "Everyone could get sick." He looked at Marge, then at Joey, and gulped. "Or even die?"

"Oh, my goodness!" Marge stood. "We must hurry."

She rushed ahead, out of the house and down the street, Joey and Seth trailing after her.

When they arrived at the green, the judges were conferring, but the entries had yet to arrive. "You two go on over to the horseshoe event; I'll meet you there," she told Joey, then she sat down with the judges and said, "We have a quandary."

Millicent Beaumonde, Mayor Wright, and the librarian, Roger Mathison, looked at her expectantly.

"I apologize before the fact, Millicent, because this involves members of your family."

"Do go on. I'm perfectly aware of their shortcomings."

"Last night, Joey and I overheard Carter coercing some boys into helping him search for buckeyes. One of the boys contacted us this morning and alleged that Carter claimed his father intends to grind them up and insert them into the chili entries."

"But why?" Millicent was horrified. "That makes no sense."

"We need a plan," Roger said.

"Whether or not the allegation is true, the most effective course of action would be preventative. However, to ensure everyone's well-being, I would like to propose a minor subterfuge."

The three judges gazed at her with varying degrees of comprehension.

"My recommendation is an eleventh-hour modification of the judges' panel. If Millicent claims she is indisposed and insists that Reginald, as a Beaumonde, must stand in, he will decline the unhealthy chili."

"What if he refuses?" Mayor Wright asked.

"I'm certain the three of you can make a compelling argument. Plan A, keep the pots covered and observe the table. Plan B, ensure Reginald is one of the judges."

Everyone agreed, and Marge set off for the horseshoe competition, calling Peter on the way.

Fabrication was unnecessary when Millicent addressed Reginald. She felt sick to her stomach when she contemplated the disastrous results of poisoned chili.

"I'll need you to represent the family for the chili competition," she told him when he stopped by the tent. "I'm feeling indisposed."

"I'm sorry, Mother, but I'm much too busy."

"We've always had a member of the Beaumonde family on the judges' panel," Roger said.

"The residents of Buckwood will be very disappointed if you don't participate," Mayor Wright added. "We need you."

"I believe that you should follow through with your obligations, Mother."

"No one will be impressed if I get sick and must leave without tasting all the chili. Think of the mess… and the gossip," Millicent countered.

Reginald shifted from one foot to the other and crossed his arms. "Fine. I'll take your place. I hope you appreciate the other duties I will have to postpone."

Once he had turned and left the tent, feigning great importance, Roger and the Mayor congratulated her. "Phase one complete," she said. "I suppose I should head home to make my excuse more plausible. Good luck with phase two."

<hr>

When Marge arrived at the horseshoe pitch, she found Seth sitting on a bench with his father and asked if she could join them. Seth's eyes darted around, looking for an escape, but Marge smiled gently and settled in to watch Joey.

"Next up, Joseph Cattywampus and Frederick Peterson," said the announcer.

Excited cheering erupted as the two main contenders accepted their horseshoes. Joey went first, throwing one ringer after another.

Cheering vociferously, Marge sat on the edge of her seat, pulse racing, as Mr. Peterson approached with his horseshoes. He appeared confident, although he must have realized the improbability of beating a perfect score. He wobbled, threw his horseshoe, put his hand on his chest, and collapsed. The horseshoe flew sideways, hitting the announcer in the head, and the assemblage froze in horror.

Joey rushed over to Mr. Peterson, pushed his walker to the side, knelt, and took his pulse. "Call an ambulance!" he shouted before grabbing the walker and heading in the direction of the announcer. The crowd around him moved back to let him through.

"Are you a doctor?" someone asked.

"No, but I served as an Army medic. Do we have a doctor available?" Everyone looked around, but no doctors came forward. Joey pushed the walker to the side again, knelt, and checked the announcer's pulse and pupils before returning to Mr. Peterson. Joey knelt and took his hand. "Hold on, Fred. Help will be here soon."

"You. Won," Mr. Peterson rasped.

"We'll have a do-over as soon as you are well enough."

"Nothing to live for now. My horseshoe days are over."

"The ambulance is here. Just hold on."

Joey indicated the two fallen men and grabbed his walker before stepping back to let the paramedics do their jobs. He stood staring at nothing for a long time.

Marge found him watching the ambulance morosely as it pulled out of the green. She stood by him silently until he turned his head and studied her.

"Where's Peter?"

Her eyes widened. "I don't know."

"Shouldn't he investigate?"

"Since Fred is still among the living and we don't know what instigated his fall, an investigation might be precipitate."

Joey looked back at the horseshoe pit and said nothing. The other spectators had moved away from the area, except for Seth. He walked up to Joey and said, "I'm sorry about your friend," and hugged him. Surprised, Joey stiffened for a moment, then hugged him back, and Marge surreptitiously wiped away a few tears with a large polyester handkerchief. She looked over at the bench and saw Seth's father waiting there.

Walking over to the bench, she sat down and said, "Your son has a big heart. Has he told you about Carter Beaumonde?"

Oliver shook his head.

"Carter has been compelling Seth to misbehave by threatening to make you redundant. You might like to cogitate a means to relieve the coercion."

Oliver looked at her oddly. "Carter is threatening to get me fired?"

"If you prefer to be direct, yes."

"And he's making Seth do something?"

"Various... things. Yes. Please don't treat him severely. He is endeavoring to protect you."

They both stood. "Thank you for letting me know. I'll talk to him over pizza this afternoon."

Marge smiled and turned toward Joey. Seth was gone, and a sense of foreboding stole over her. "You should locate him promptly," she said over her shoulder and began to chew on her cuticles.

"Let's go check out the chili competition," Joey said as he approached her. "Why are you biting your fingers?"

"How long ago did Seth leave? I was speaking with his father."

"I don't know. Carter and the boys were hanging around. I think he was trying to avoid them. Did you tell Oliver what's been going on?"

"I didn't provide specifics."

"Good."

Marge glanced at him. "Are you alright?"

He swallowed. "I'm fine. Fred will be fine." Nodding emphatically, he said, "Let's go see about the chili."

Chapter 10

A crowd had formed around the judges' tent at the cookoff. Reginald Beaumonde sat with Mayor Wright and Roger Mathison. He wore a strained look as he watched the servers bring unidentifiable cups of chili from the multitude of pots on the far table. Each cup bore a number that could later be associated with a pot of chili.

"I wonder how confident Roger and the Mayor are that no one tampered with the chili."

"They don't look as nervous as Reginald."

Harriet, wearing a prim, floral sundress and cardigan, took up the microphone. "Ladies and gentlemen, welcome to the 5th annual chili cookoff." A cheer rose from the crowd, and Reginald wiped his brow with a silk handkerchief. "This year will be challenging for the judges because we have no less than twenty entries!" More cheering. "Each cup is numbered to correspond with the pot it was poured from, and the judges will make notes and sip milk in between to cleanse their palates. Now, let us meet our judges." Harriet walked over to the mayor. "Our first judge is Mayor Gladys Wright, a first-time cookoff judge."

Mayor Wright stood, looking sharp in black slacks and a pink and white striped shirt, her salt and pepper hair peeking out from beneath a jaunty pink hat. "Thank you, everyone. I am extremely excited to taste all these wonderful recipes."

"Our second judge is Roger Mathison, Librarian, a third-year veteran."

Roger held up his hand to the applause. "Thank you. Glad to be here."

"And finally, standing in for his mother-in-law, we have Reginald Beaumonde. Thank you for the assist, Reginald."

55

"Anything for the community," he croaked, looking slightly green.

"The rules are: first, second, and third prizes will be chosen subjectively by the judges. If there is a tie, all three judges will try the two chilis in question and vote again. There will be no arguing about the results. The judges' decisions are final. Please return for your opportunity to sample the entries in one hour."

One might have expected a stampede, but the entire audience stayed where they were, expecting the sampling to provide some amusement and stories to tell. Marge and Joey watched the judges carefully.

Reginald kept leaning over and trying to see which chili Roger was eating, but he carefully turned his cups so Reginald couldn't see the numbers. At one point, the mayor bit into a hot pepper, turned red, and started sipping milk at a startling pace. Reginald spit something back into the cup it came from.

"I wonder if that chili had something crunchy in it." Joey elbowed Marge.

"Shh."

Finally, the judges finished sampling all the cups except for one, which sat in front of Reginald, labeled B.

"What's that, Reggie? Are you going to try it?" Roger asked.

"No, and please don't call me Reggie." He shook his head.

"Why not?"

"That's not my name."

"I mean, why aren't you going to try it?"

"It doesn't have a number on it. What does B mean?"

"Maybe it's thirteen. You should sample it."

"You sample it if you want. I have accounted for twenty cups of chili."

The judges handed their tally sheets to Pastor Greg, who added up the scores and passed them to Harriet. "Ladies and Gentlemen, we have our winners."

As Harriet was reading off the winners to loud cheering, and spectators were lining up for a chance to sample the entries, Sergeant Peter Locke approached Reginald and put a hand on his shoulder. "If you could come with me, Mr. Beaumonde, we won't need to make a scene."

Joey purchased a ten-cup sample pack, which included salad and French bread. Marge chose the five-cup pack and looked through the entries for those which contained smaller quantities of beans. She was salivating from the smell of beef, onions, chili powder, and myriad secret ingredients, but there was an unpleasant, unidentifiable whiff in the air underlying the fragrant chilis. She wrinkled her nose and tried to ignore it, but once she had noticed it, she couldn't not smell it. Roger and Gladys pulled up chairs and joined them when the crowd had thinned out.

"How did you pull that off?" Joey asked around bites.

"It was Millicent's idea." Roger grinned. "We took one cup of chili from each entry and put them in five pots labeled A to D. All the entries were covered and placed under the table, but pots A-D were left open on the top. We took turns watching and saw Reginald put something in the pots, stir them, and leave the tent. Once he left, we removed the tainted pots and put the real entries on the table. Since judging was blind, Reginald had no idea how to identify which chili was poisoned."

"Who gave him the extra cup from B?"

Roger frowned. "That I don't know. But since he refused to taste it, we can give the police the contents of pot B for evidence."

"I would recommend disposing of the contaminated chili to prevent accidental ingestion," Marge said.

"Don't worry. We have. Thank you for saving the cookoff," the mayor said. "I have to go judge the 4-H pig competition now." She stood and gave them a little wave before heading across the green.

That's the smell. "Where are the 4-H pens, Roger?"

"They're off behind the stage. You smell it too."

"Yes, the breeze is traveling in an unfortunate direction."

<hr>

Peter sat in the interview room at the station, nervously facing Reginald Beaumonde. "The cook-off judges were informed of your plan to poison the chili entries and took steps to ensure everyone's safety. They witnessed you putting what were presumably buckeyes into the decoy pots and have submitted those pots for testing. Would you like to make a statement?"

"They are lying, and I have nothing further to say until my attorney is present."

Peter nodded and asked the deputy to return him to his cell.

Stopping Peter on his way out, the chief said, "What is the meaning of this, Locke?"

"Reginald poisoned the chili entries in front of witnesses, and I believe he could also be responsible for the other incidents of vandalism around town."

"Do you have any idea how preposterous that sounds? Do you have any evidence to back up this theory of yours?"

"Yes, sir. The chili is being tested, and we're looking for the little girl who dropped the bacon on the tables on Friday."

"You had better tread lightly, Locke, or your career will be over."

"I understand, sir."

Practically hyperventilating, Peter left the station and sat in his cruiser until his heart rate returned to normal.

<hr>

"I'm feeling a little tired."

"It has been an eventful morning. Shall we take our repose?"

Joey nodded. "Get our second wind.".

Wind. I'll need some Bean-o when I get home.

The walk home did them both good, and they planned to meet again in two hours. Marge entered her house and navigated directly to the kitchen cabinet for her chili-bean antidote. *Maybe I should suggest a spaghetti cookoff next year. What should I make for the potluck?*

Upstairs, she removed her shoes and lay down on her bed for a short rest and was jolted awake by sharp knocking on her front door. Looking at her bedside clock, she was surprised to see two hours had passed. "Just a minute," she yelled. "Coming." She grabbed her shoes, ran downstairs, and flung open the front door. Joey, she expected, but Peter was standing with him on the porch. "Sorry, I fell asleep. What are you doing here, Petey?"

Peter eyed her bun. *Did it just move?* He tore his eyes away. "I finished interviewing Reginald. His hearing is set for Monday, and he's out on bail. I understand that it was you who initially warned the judges, so I'll need to interview you as well."

"We were about to return to the green. May we postpone?"

"Yes, I suppose. Before Monday." He glanced at her hair again. "I'll catch up with you later." He glanced at Joey, who was also staring at Marge's large, curly bun.

"Thanks, Petey." Marge smiled and patted her hair, then stopped with her hand raised. "I'll be right back."

The two of them watched her race upstairs.

Joey's shoulders shook with mirth at Peter's raised eyebrows. "I imagine she'll be a few minutes, so you can go ahead and get back to the station. We'll find you later so you can interview her."

"Thank you," Peter said uncertainly, looking toward the stairs as he left.

Marge raced to the restroom and looked in the mirror. "Oh, my." She felt around in her enormous curly bun and pulled out her mouse, Fergus. "What are you doing in there?" Finding his cage on its side with the door open, she suspected Fluster had been on the prowl. "Poor little guy. I'm sorry Fluster is so naughty. Let's keep the door closed this afternoon." She put him gently in his righted cage and closed the door to her bedroom. "Fluster," she called. "Fluuster." She returned to her room, remembering that she needed to rearrange her bun, and discovered the cat on top of Fergus' cage. "Out." She pointed to the door. "Out you go." Fluffing and rearranging her hair, she left her room a second time and firmly shut the door. "I'm sorry, Joey. Are you ready?"

"Yes." His eyes were filled with merriment. "Anything you want to talk about?"

"All is well." She laughed, patting her bun to be sure.

Chapter 11

Walking silently toward the green, they observed a sizeable crowd of costumed people milling about. Marge bent down and picked up a long, decorated stick. "Look at this, Joey. Isn't it beautiful?" She hoisted it in the air and heard band instruments, so she pretended she was leading a marching band. Up and down, she thrust the stick in the air, marching in time to It's a Grand Old Flag. The crowd parted, providing Joey a glimpse of the bemused-looking band teacher standing on the sidewalk.

When they reached the green, Marge veered to the right, cutting through the grass toward the afternoon exhibits, followed by the entire high school marching band. Their teacher, running to intercept her, cried, "Stop. Stop!"

"Marge, you're going to have to give the stick back."

"Why? I'm having so much fun."

"Look behind you."

Marge turned and gaped. The teacher, skidding to a stop in front of her, said, "You did a marvelous job, Ms. Bumfuzzle, but I'm afraid we must rejoin the parade now."

She grinned. "Thank you for allowing me the opportunity. It was a thrilling experience." She handed him the baton, and he raised it high before leading the band back to the street. "I wonder why it was lying on the ground. How exhilarating."

Joey, who had seen the drum major throw it down before stomping off in a pique of frustration, smiled silently and allowed Marge her miracle.

❦

Scanning the myriad rides, Marge said, "Should we buy tickets or get bracelets?"

"This is our designated ride day, so let's get bracelets. We can ride until we're sick."

"Rides don't make us sick." She elbowed him. "Except those baskets that go upside down, and that was only once, really."

Joey turned a little green, and his stomach flipped, as he vividly recalled the ride. *That was so disgusting.* "Let's not try that one today."

"I'm sure that was just because of the spicy lunch, but if it concerns you, there are plenty of other rides." They stood in line to purchase their ride bracelets and again to ride the Ferris wheel. Once seated, they crept upward at a painstakingly slow pace while the carnie seated passengers one car at a time. They had plenty of time to look out over the green and watch their friends and neighbors enjoying themselves.

Marge concentrated on the lovely afternoon, one of those days when colors seem especially vibrant, the sun shines brightly, and the birds are chirping.

"Marge? Marge."

Snapping out of her reverie, she looked inquiringly at Joey. "I'm sorry. Could you repeat that?"

"I've been talking for several minutes, but the last part was, 'Would you like to have lunch now?'"

"Oh, yes. Not something spicy because… you know."

Disembarking from the Ferris Wheel, Joey grinned. "The ride with the baskets. How about those gyros?"

"They aren't spicy?" Marge said as they walked toward the food trucks.

"I don't think so. Would you rather have something else?"

"No, let's try the gyros. We just won't ride in the baskets."

"I thought we had already agreed not to ride them."

"Oh. I suppose we did. Let's ask the chef if we can exchange ingredients before we get our gyros. It won't be as messy."

"Let's each get two. They don't look very big, and we can try different kinds."

"That's a great idea. I didn't think of that."

Joey placed their order at the window, and by the time they found a table, their number was called. Marge went to get their plates and had pop on her blouse before she returned. Setting the tray in the middle of the table and sitting across from Joey, she picked up a gyro. "Bon Appetit," she said before taking a large bite. Chewing twice, stopping, chewing twice more, she stopped and made a face.

"What's the matter?" Joey paused with his gyro not quite in his mouth.

Marge finished chewing, swallowed, and grimaced. "I might have an aversion to lamb."

Joey looked at his wrapper. "This is the lamb. Let me try it." He took a small bite and chewed. Then he took another. "It's different, but I kind of like it."

"If you want to take the onions off, you can have mine too."

"You should take half of my chicken then."

Marge picked up her chicken and took a bite, nodding as she chewed. "Much better."

<hr />

The bell on the door tinkled when Peter strolled into the café. He studied Sally, standing at the cash register, watching her customers for signs of want. Roger peered into his coffee cup and set it down. Harriet scanned vacant tables, hoping to spy a stray ketchup bottle, Pastor Greg set his menu on the table, all obvious clues, but Sally straightened her uniform and smiled brightly, giving Peter her undivided attention. "Well, hello, officer. How can I help you?"

Peter guessed she was several years his junior. He was approaching thirty and painfully shy around attractive young women.

Sally was willowy with strawberry blonde hair and a mischievous smile. *You could go out with me.* "Could I get a coffee to go, please?"

"Of course. Two creams and two sugars?"

"Yes, please." *She knows my order. Why do I get so tongue tied? Ask her out already.* "Um, Sally?"

She turned toward him expectantly, but the bell jangled again, and Reginald Beaumonde strode in with purpose. Sally frowned.

"Could we have a word?"

"Sorry, Peter. Coffee's on the house today. I hope you'll stop by later." She handed him his coffee and walked toward the back door with Reginald.

Peter's heart sank. *Not Sally. Why can't that old reprobate stay in his own pasture?*

Rather than walk all the way home for a rest, Marge and Joey decided to lie down in the grass beneath a weeping willow tree. "This was such a wonderful idea, Joey. It feels like our own little fairy world. If we had a few twinkling lights, it would be perfect."

Joey's eyes crinkled merrily. "I don't know if people forget the hollow behind the flowing branches or if they don't enter because they fear the unknown. Maybe both."

Marge closed her eyes, and her lips turned up slightly. "Tell me when break time is over."

Joey closed his eyes for a few minutes, but he was unable to relax under the willow tree, so he looked at his watch. Making himself vulnerable in such a place was like sleeping in a cave. Something could enter, but you'd never see it coming.

He was right, of course. Just before he woke Marge, a group of boys sped through the willow tree boughs on their bicycles. Joey stood in front of Marge's prone, sleeping body, put out his hand, and yelled, "halt!"

The boys hit their brakes, ran into each other, skidded on the grass, and one even ran into the tree trunk. "Hey. Now, look what you did, old man. You owe us all new bicycles."

"No, I saved you from going to jail for killing a sleeping woman. If you had been careful, realizing that someone else might be under this tree, you wouldn't have had that accident."

"I'm going to tell my dad."

"Good; tell him to contact Sergeant Locke at the police station to sign his statement, and be sure to let the sergeant know you almost ran over his aunt."

The boy frowned and picked up his bike. All the bicycles were still in working order except for the one that hit the tree. The handlebars were not quite straight on that one. After the boys left, Joey approached Marge. *How did she sleep through all that?* As he approached, she sat up and laughed.

"Have you been awake this whole time?"

"No one could sleep through that."

"Why didn't you say something?"

"I didn't want to interrupt. I thought it might lessen the impact of your message."

Joey snorted as he proffered a hand to help her up. "I'm hungry again."

"Let's ride a couple terrifying rides first… before, you know."

"Sounds reasonable. Which ones are the scariest?"

"That one." Marge pointed as they ducked from underneath the branches.

"That's just a little rollercoaster."

"Appearances can be deceiving." She grabbed his walker and led him to the entrance booth. There was no line, so Joey left his walker with the young man running the ride and climbed into the car with Marge.

"When Peter was little, we came to the festival and rode this rollercoaster. 'If you feel scared, just yell as loud as you can,' I told him. We still yell if we ride together."

"Let's yell then. Is it scary enough to make us yell?"

"It is if you have a bad back."

The old, metal cars began to move forward along the wood and metal tracks. Clackety-clackety-clackety, slow and rough, up the first small hill. Once the cars reached the top, gravity increased their momentum, and they whipped through the first twisty turn at an extraordinary speed. The close, sharp turns on the small track, combined with the jerking movement of the cars and the unexpected velocity, were frightening. Joey had no problem keeping his end of the bargain. When they pulled to a stop, he looked at Marge and said, "Now that's what they call hair raising."

His smirk worried Marge, who slowly put a hand up to her giant curly bun. "What happened?"

"It's not bad. It just seems to have grown about two inches."

"Ooh. I need to see this. Where can I find a mirror?"

"There's the funhouse over there."

They walked through the funhouse, posing before the strangely shaped mirrors. One of the mirrors provided a long, narrow reflection, and Marge could see her exaggeratedly tall, cylindrical bun perched atop her head. "Now, isn't that fascinating? Is that an accurate depiction?"

"Not exactly," Joey admitted, laughing. "This mirror takes some liberties."

"I'll take another look at it when we get to the Fireside. Are you ready?"

"May I take a photograph of your hair?" He pulled out his phone.

Marge smiled and struck a pose. "Now I won't need a mirror. May I see it?"

"You're a good sport." He laughed as she studied the picture. "Can we eat now?"

"Yes. Victuals are in order. Perhaps we will acquire information at the café. The pie competition will transpire this afternoon, so take care not to overindulge."

"Did you enter?"

"No, but that reminds me; I must elect my contribution to the potluck and obtain the ingredients. Any requests?"

"I'll think about it while we eat. Right now, I could eat anything."

Chapter 12

Marge pulled the door to the Fireside Café open with vigor, causing the bell to clang rather than ding. "Hello, Ms. Bumfuzzle. Mr. Cattywampus." Sally greeted them with her usual cheer.

"Hello, Sally," Marge said over her shoulder as she strode to the center table with purpose. The café was close to capacity, the noise level deafening.

Following with menus and a smile, Sally waited for them to get seated, then placed their menus on the table. "Would you like something to drink?"

"I think I would like an iced tea."

Joey raised his eyebrows. "I'll have one too."

"I'll be back in a moment to take your order."

"What's the occasion?"

"Shh. Let's just listen for a moment." Marge closed her eyes and concentrated, waiting for the gossip to envelop her.

"Sally and Reginald were out back."

"Dead body in the bathroom."

"He claimed he was cheated."

"Having an affair."

"She wins every year. I think it's fixed."

"Milk plant will shut down."

Sally returned with the drinks, pulling Marge from her reverie. "Are you ready to order?"

"What's the special today?" Joey asked.

"It's a fried chicken bowl. Creamy mashed potatoes topped with small pieces of fried chicken, corn, gravy, and shredded cheese."

"Comfort food. I'll have that." Marge picked up her tea and took a sip.

"Me too." Joey nodded. After Sally bustled to the kitchen to place their order, he said, "Is everything okay?"

Marge smiled briefly but didn't answer immediately. "It's the gossip," she said finally. "There's something unpleasant unfolding and it has me concerned."

The bell on the door jingled, and Peter entered, looking around briefly before approaching their table. He glanced at Marge's hair but didn't comment. "May I join you?"

"Of course," Marge said absently. "Do you have an update on Mr. Peterson's condition?"

"He had a heart attack, but he reached the hospital in time. He's recuperating in ICU."

"That's great. I told him I'd give him a rematch when he's discharged. I should visit once he gets out of ICU."

Peter looked up and smiled at Sally's approach. "Is that the special?"

"Yes, shall I bring one more?" Her eyes twinkled.

"Yes, please."

"Anything to drink?"

"Water will be fine. Thank you."

Sally swished away toward the kitchen.

Marge glanced at Joey and took a bite of chicken. Joey took a bite too. They both chewed and looked around.

"This is delicious." She took a sip of her tea.

"I agree." Joey took another bite.

They both watched Peter, who didn't seem to notice they were sitting with him.

<hr>

When Sally returned to her post at the cash register, Peter stood and, taking a deep breath, approached the counter.

"Did you need anything else?" she asked.

"Yes, actually." He cleared his throat. "I would like to invite you to dinner when you're free." Peter was perspiring slightly and had to resist the urge to look at his shoes.

"How lovely. I'll give you my number, and we can talk about it when I get off work."

Her smile made Peter's knees weak. *She said yes. Oh my god. She said yes!* They exchanged numbers, and he returned to the table, where he sat staring at his phone in a daze. He hadn't touched his food when Marge and Joey stood.

"It was lovely having lunch with you, Petey, but we must be on our way."

Peter looked up, glanced at his bowl, and blushed. "I'm sorry, Aunt Marge. I'll be better company next time."

———— •·⤜✦⤛·• ————

"Ah, to be young," Joey said.

"We remain young at heart."

They paid at the register and left the café, nearly colliding with Millicent, who was hurrying along the sidewalk with a grocery bag.

"Oh! Excuse me. I didn't mean to cause an accident."

"Please don't fret. You are always so organized; I don't believe I've ever seen you rushing."

"You know, I told you I bought ingredients for my souffle? Someone has used the entire block of cheese. I had to visit the grocer again before I can begin cooking."

"Don't let us keep you. I'm looking forward to that souffle." Joey smiled.

Millicent continued on her way, although less hastily, and Marge said, "Don't let me forget to purchase provisions before the grocer puts up the shutters."

"Yes, ma'am." He winked. "Let's cross here."

Walking across the green, Marge looked up and watched a few fluffy white clouds float slowly across the bright blue sky.

Then she stopped, her attention drawn to the top of the Ferris wheel. "Do you have your binoculars?"

Joey dug around in his pockets for a compact set, unsurprised to see Marge perched on the large limb of a nearby tree. He handed her the binoculars, and she rose to her knees, straining for a better view. Once she had accomplished her task, she handed the binoculars back and slipped, hanging from the branch by one bent leg and waving her arms about. Joey tried to stop her fall but, as was wont to occur, she landed on him, knocking him down in the process.

⸙

Choosing that moment to walk by Pastor Greg stopped and gawked.

"Could you give me a hand, Pastor? I must reach the Ferris wheel."

He helped her up and watched her sprint across the green, shook his head, and offered Joey a hand. "What's going on over there?"

"I'm not sure." Joey looked across at Marge, waving her arms and pointing at the top of the Ferris wheel, where two people stood, struggling. He pulled out his phone and dialed Peter's number as he and Greg headed in Marge's direction. "Peter, I think we have a situation on the Ferris wheel."

"I see it. I'm on my way. Thanks."

Marge was standing at the base of the Ferris wheel, arguing with the complacent ride operator, when Joey and Pastor Greg caught up with her.

"I understand, ma'am, but if I speed it up, I won't be able to stop it," he said reasonably.

"At least stop loading passengers."

"We'll want to keep it going after we get those two off." He surreptitiously backed away as her anxiety became self-evident.

"If one of them is pushed, it will be murder, and you'll be shut down for the next month," Peter said as he approached. "Get them down here now." He grimaced and glanced at Marge.

The operator shrugged and slowly lowered the top car to ground level. James Nelson and Oliver Drake, who had been grappling seconds earlier, suddenly sat still in their seats, red in the face and breathing hard.

"Would the two of you like to explain why you are holding up the Ferris wheel?"

"No, we'll just leave," James said.

"I don't think so. Disturbing the peace and assault. We'll all be paying a visit to the station. Come with me, please."

"Can I start the wheel back up?"

"Yes. Go ahead. Thank you for your assistance."

"Do you two want a ride since I have an extra bucket?"

"Sure. Come on, Marge, let's take a ride."

The Ferris wheel ride helped Marge clear her head. "Joey. Why were Oliver and James skirmishing?"

"What?" He yelled. For some reason, the ride seemed extremely noisy. *The combination of the wind and voices carrying, I suppose.*

Marge leaned in and spoke in his ear, repeating her question.

"I don't know. It seemed serious, though. I imagine Peter will sort it out."

"Do you think James will be present at the milk plant tonight?"

Joey leaned in, too, attempting to understand what she was saying. "I have no idea." They had gone around the loop several times, and the wind was beginning to make Joey nervous. Looking down, he saw the operator flirting with someone in sandals and a skirt. He turned to tell Marge, but she had already seen and was rummaging in her pockets. Holding up her treasure, a shiny penny, she leaned forward and dropped it. They watched it fall in slow motion, then sonic speed, as it dropped between the operator and his friend and bounced to a stop at their feet.

Looking up, the operator saw Marge make a large X with her arms in front of her, so he slowed the wheel when her bucket approached.

"Is something wrong?"

"Yes, we have circled sufficiently. The wind is becoming uncomfortable."

"Anyone else want off?"

Someone in the crowded waiting line said, "Some of us would like to get on."

With a slight shrug, the operator began unloading the cars.

Joey shook his head after they disembarked. "That was a good trick."

"The penny?"

"Yes. He wouldn't have heard if we had yelled.

Chapter 13

Sitting in the greenish-gray interview room at the police station, Peter interviewed Oliver and James separately. He began with James since he knew him slightly, and as they sat at the small white table in hard white chairs, he began to feel depressed, his eyes glazing over. *Why am I here? Doing this? My whole life is spent with criminals.*

"Sergeant? Are you okay?" James leaned his bulk forward with concern.

"I'm fine." He shook himself. "What was your fight about? Why were you and Oliver even on the Ferris wheel together?"

"We didn't want to be overheard."

"And the fight?"

James groaned and ran a large hand through his unruly hair. "It was so stupid." He put his elbows on the table and hung his head.

Peter sat and waited, carefully watching James's body language.

He finally pushed himself up and looked at Peter. "I accused him of lying about what I reported at the plant and getting me fired. I wanted to know why. The stupid part is that I brought up his wife." He hung his head again.

"What about his wife?"

"I thought everyone knew. It's all over town."

"James," Peter said sternly.

"His wife is having an affair with Reginal Beaumonde. He knew about the affair; he just didn't know who."

"What exactly did you say?"

"I told him I needed that job to finish the payments on an engagement ring for Freida. And he said not to bother. She'd just walk out on me someday and break my heart.

I got angry and said if she did, I sure wouldn't keep working for her lover." He looked at Peter with wide eyes and whispered, "You should have seen him. I thought he was going to kill me."

"Everyone has their limits. You pushed him too far. I will let you apologize after I speak with him."

Peter banged on the door and asked the guard to return James to his cell and deliver Oliver.

Oliver Drake walked in a defeated man. He plopped onto the hard white chair without even a wince.

"James explained to me what happened and what was said. Could I hear your version?"

"I don't even care. Whatever he said is fine."

"He basically said that he went too far and made you so angry he thought you were going to kill him."

"The ridiculous part is that I wasn't mad at James. I was mad because Reginald and my wife have been making a fool of me, and the whole town knew, except me. I didn't get him fired, by the way."

Peter nodded, stood, and banged on the door. "Bring James back, please," he told the deputy.

James re-entered the interview room, and Peter said, "Tell Oliver what you told me."

The giant of a man looked contrite. "I'm sorry. I shouldn't have opened my big trap."

"And what did you tell me, Oliver?"

"I wasn't mad at you; I was mad about the situation."

"You sure acted mad."

"I was. It was just misdirected."

"The reason I want you both here is because I need to issue you a warning. What you did could have had serious consequences, not only for you but for others around you. Imagine if one of you had fallen and landed on someone, a child, for example. Or what if you landed right in front of a child, all messy and horrifying? You could have given him or her a lifetime of therapy."

Oliver and James gaped at Peter and then at each other.

"You got lucky this time. No one got hurt. Next time, you might not have the same luck."

"It will never happen again, Sergeant."

"Absolutely not." James nodded.

"Because you have assured me that you understand, you are free to go."

They didn't dawdle.

Jenny, the deputy who manned the front desk, popped her head around the corner. "Sally Drake is here with coffee." She raised her eyebrows.

Peter smiled. "That is good news."

Sally was shown in and sat in the chair across from Peter. She handed him his coffee and studied his face. "You're having a hard time." There was no question or censure. She simply stated an observation.

How does she know? I don't want to say too much before we even go on a date.

"Do you want to talk about it?"

"Yes. No. I don't know what my problem is."

"You probably do if you really think about it."

"I love my job, and I think I'm pretty good at it, but this evening, all of a sudden, it felt really depressing."

"It's a hard sort of job, isn't it? You always see everyone at their worst. I couldn't do it."

"You could. You're a rock. And you're very intelligent."

"What makes you say that?"

"Which one?"

"Both." She leaned forward with a serious look on her face.

He put his hand on hers. "I know you're a rock because you are always listening to other people's problems. You give them emotional support when they need it.

That's more difficult than what I do. I don't have to be empathetic with my criminals."

She was gazing into his eyes, and he almost lost his train of thought.

"The intelligent part is obvious. Your memory is amazing, you do complicated sums in your head, you can talk on almost any topic, and your advice is sound."

"Do you mean all that?"

"I don't have the imagination to make it up."

"That is probably the nicest thing anyone has ever said to me, well, all those things you said. Men often think that complimenting my appearance will please me, but complimenting my mind or my character shows that you are paying attention to me, not just my outer shell."

"Outer shells change. It's important to be with someone you appreciate for their whole self. Look at my Aunt Marge and Joey. They aren't romantically involved, but they could be. They are best friends and so much more to each other than a surface attraction. I hope I have a best friend like that when I'm their age."

"Have either of them been married?"

"Joey was. When he returned from the war, his wife was frightened by his nightmares, I think. Aunt Marge's first fiancé died, and her second left her at the altar. She decided she wasn't meant for marriage. I think they like their current arrangement. They have companionship but also independence."

"Is that what you want too?"

"No. I'm young enough that I want it all."

Sally smiled. "Me too. I should get back to work."

"Thank you for coming. I appreciate the coffee, but talking to you really helped. I'm looking forward to our date."

"It can't be much better than this, except maybe for a kiss at the end." She winked, and Peter blushed.

Chapter 14

Choosing some tamer rides after lunch, Marge and Joey made good use of their bracelets. "Which was your favorite?" Marge asked.

"I really enjoyed that one." Joey pointed to a ride that had individual swings on long chains. As the ride gathered speed, the swings soared ever higher.

"I like that one too. I felt like I was flying." She tilted her head. "Maybe we should try skydiving."

"Aren't we a little old for that?"

"You're only as old as you feel."

Joey looked at his watch. "I *feel* like eating pie right now. The judging has already started."

"Lead the way."

The pie competition was in the same tent used for the chili cookoff. Not everyone makes chili, but the people of Buckwood love their pies. The overabundance of entries required categories and multiple panels of judges. The categories were fruit, berry, meringue, meat pies, and others, including vegetable and nut pies.

Entering the tent, Marge looked around and said, "How will we ever choose? There must be close to 100."

"I'll pick my favorites."

"Rhubarb is my favorite, but I also love lemon meringue and fresh strawberry."

"Maybe we can get extra to take home. I wonder if they have a limit." Joey looked like a kid in a candy store. Choosing seven kinds of pie and accepting a box to carry them in, he glanced at Marge, who chose three. "If you can't eat those, I am willing to help."

"You have plenty. Kindly refrain from pilfering mine."

79

"Just offering. I have a box, you know." Joey snickered.

The long picnic tables and benches sitting around the perimeter of the tent were nearly full, so Marge and Joey squeezed in between Roger and Mayor Wright. Sitting across from them were Harriet and Pastor Greg. Harriet, whose husband had passed away a decade before, was besotted by the pastor. She took an extremely active role in church events, sat next to him at Bible study, and touched his hands and arms whenever possible. Greg, on the other hand, tried his best to discourage her without dampening her spiritual fervor. Each time she scooted closer to him, he slid slightly in the other direction until he couldn't slide any further without sitting on his neighbor's lap.

Harriet had one piece of apple pie, and she stared at Joey's box in amazement. "What on earth are you going to do with all that pie?"

"I plan to eat it, either in this sitting or the next." He grinned.

"We might be due for a sermon on gluttony."

Greg, who had four pieces of pie on his own plate, cleared his throat. "I believe pie contests are exempt." He hid his smile at Harriet's outrage.

"Did you enter a pie?" Marge asked kindly.

"Yes, this one." She stabbed her piece of apple pie.

"I must try it. Do you know the number?"

"Twelve."

Marge got up and walked to the pie display, returning with a piece of apple pie. She took a big bite and pasted a wide smile on her face as she chewed.

Joey saved her by changing the subject. "Has anyone heard how Mr. Peterson is doing? Last I heard, he was in the ICU."

Carefully burying the apple pie under stray pieces of crust, Marge finished most of her favorites and escaped with Joey before Harriet could interrogate her. They walked back toward the rides.

"Was it that bad?" he asked finally.

"I am not a big fan of apple anyway, but Joey, the apples were hard and sour, and the crust tasted like store-bought. I was petrified she was going to ask me how it tasted, and I couldn't produce a positive and encouraging rejoinder on the spot."

"You could tell her it tasted very fresh and ask her for the recipe."

"Excellent. I should hire you as my PR expert."

"At your service." He bowed. "What shall we ride first?"

"I can't believe you are ambulatory after all that pie."

Shrugging and looking slightly sheepish, he said, "I only finished three. The other four are in the box."

"Three are plausible. I ate three and feel too full, but not sick."

"Are you too full to ride the Ferris wheel again?"

"The Ferris wheel might be about my speed right now."

<hr>

Upon returning from her lawyer's office, Millicent slowly walked up the long staircase and entered the guest room. She sat on the edge of the bed where Gavin had slept, now perfectly made, and gave some serious thought as to whether or not Elizabeth or Reginald might have harmed him. Her immediate response to Peter was, of course not, but if one of them thought Gavin posed a risk to their inheritance, she couldn't guarantee that they would not react. Saddened by the thought, and the lost opportunity to get to know her son, Millicent said a prayer for her family, especially for her grandchildren, who were being raised with a love of money and a lack of moral compass. That afternoon she had overheard a conversation between a young man and his son regarding Carter's bullying, and her granddaughter, Ellie, was so self-involved that she couldn't attend a family dinner once a week. *Please, Lord, let them feel your presence and do thy will.* Feeling suddenly weary, she went to her own room for a short nap. She surprised herself by locking the door and wondered when she had started doing that.

"The ride bracelets haven't expired, but unbelievably, I feel all rode out."

"I concur. I must reach the grocery store before they close. It's only six, so maybe we could call the pizza place, head to the grocery, and be home in time for dinner."

"Sounds good. Do you want me to call while you shop?"

"Exceptional synchronization. I'll return momentarily."

Marge's 'momentarily' was subjective, but Joey was prepared for that. He didn't call the pizza parlor until he saw her in line. He ordered her favorite pizza and was waiting to help her carry groceries when she exited the store.

"I apologize for my delay. The stocker was required to comb the cache in the back to unearth the requisite ingredients."

"I understand. I took the appropriate measures." Ignoring her startled look with a smile, Joey grabbed the heaviest bags and hung them over his handlebars. The ten-minute walk home wore him out, but he waited patiently while Marge whipped together her potluck offering, then sat down with her in the kitchen.

She opened the pizza box and gaped at the pie. "What is this?"

Joey peeked into the box. "Well, I'm not sure. It's not what I ordered."

Marge read the tag on the side of the box. *Chicken, artichoke hearts, and white sauce.* "Hm. It smells pretty good."

"I wouldn't know."

"Let's try it. If it's terrible, we can add some jalapeños or barbecue sauce or something."

Each taking a bite, they chewed and nodded, savoring the alien taste and finding it acceptable.

"I don't mind it at all," Marge said, finally.

"Not bad. I was trying to order your favorite, though. I'll have to have a word with Norris. He doesn't usually make such huge mistakes."

"It's not terrible, but you might want to let him know about the mix-up, just for future reference. You know, I think this is our fourth or fifth meal today. I'm not actually hungry yet. What time are we supposed to be at the milk plant?"

"Not until one, and we have church in the morning. Should we take a nap?"

"That's a splendid idea; then we will relish the pizza when we rise. What time should we set our alarms for?"

Joey thought about that. "We don't want to be late, and we want to make time for coffee and pizza and getting over there. Eleven?"

"Come over at eleven. I think I'll aim for ten-thirty. Sometimes rousing myself is a struggle when I'm sleeping soundly."

Joey stood. "Sounds like a good plan. See you at eleven."

Marge saw him to the door and locked it, flipping the two deadbolts for good measure. She turned out all the lights except the one in the kitchen, then trudged upstairs to her room. As exhaustion overtook her, Marge laid down on her bed, forgetting to set her alarm, and was sound asleep within seconds.

Chapter 15

Joey walked across the street and let himself into his chilly house. He had turned the heat down when he left in the morning and didn't see the point of turning it back on for just a few hours. Setting his alarm, he climbed into bed and pulled his heavy blankets up to his chin. Although he was in no hurry to greet his nightmares, his eyelids felt heavy, and he quickly drifted off to sleep.

Trying to claw his way out of a foxhole filled with dead soldiers, Joey heard the air siren and smelled burning flesh, his nose and mouth filled with dust and chemicals. Assailed by fear, heart racing, he ranger crawled to the door and checked the handle to see if it was hot. "Clear!" He opened the door and crawled out. Once his hands touched the cold tile of the front entrance, he realized he was in his own home and he was safe. His alarm was blaring. A good time to get up. Dressing rapidly in all black, he let himself out the front door and rushed across the street to the warmth and safety of Marge's house.

He knocked politely at her front door, but she didn't answer. He knocked louder and finally rang the bell. Frowning, he rang three short bursts and again waited. *She forgot to set her alarm.* He sighed. He had his own key, but that was for emergencies. *Is this an emergency?* He leaned on the doorbell once again.

⁂

Marge was back in school, attempting to keep order in a classroom full of twenty-five noisy, unruly teenagers. They laughed and threw paper airplanes while she was trying to explain an important grammatical concept.

Her face grew increasingly red with her frustration, and just as she was about to erupt into an inappropriate diatribe, the school bell began to ring. It rang and rang, turning into the fire bell. Shooing her students out of the classroom, she looked down to discover Fluster biting her bare feet.

"Why are you biting my feet?" she said, finally waking up and realizing the ringing was her doorbell. Looking at her bedside clock, she saw it was eleven o'clock, so she jumped out of bed, tripped over Fluster, and slid across the floor. Scrambling to her feet, she raced down the stairs and yanked the front door open.

Joey stood on the doorstep, grinning. "Good thing you didn't change into your negligée."

"The students would have been traumatized. I'm so relieved I'm retired."

Initially confused, Joey's face registered his understanding. "Another teaching nightmare." He nodded with compassion. "Let's put on some coffee. How did you put up with the little beasts for so long?"

Marge led the way into the kitchen, where she began preparing a pot of coffee. "I enjoyed teaching elementary school." Her brow furrowed. "The torture began when I started teaching remedial English at the high school. Those kids had endured years of humiliation and gave as good as they got. They absolutely reveled in the opportunity to mock me."

"I was locked in my nightmares when my alarm went off as well. Being pulled from that hell wasn't all bad." He smiled gently.

"I'm sorry. I imagine your nightmares are far worse than mine."

He shook his head. "Our nightmares prey on our fears and insecurities. They can't be compared. Yours are just as valid as mine."

Marge turned and hugged him. She held on for a moment, then said, "Do you want your pizza warmed or cold?"

"Cold pizza and hot coffee sound great."

After several cups of coffee and two slices of pizza, Marge excused herself to change. She went upstairs to wash her face and brush her teeth, changing into an all-black ensemble like Joey's. She pondered his words as she changed. "Our nightmares prey on our fears and insecurities," he had said. Marge had taken the high school teaching position shortly after being diagnosed with an allergy to natural fibers, and her anxiety-induced flatulence increased with her students' mockery. As a teacher who strove to make a difference, she understood the root of their disinterest and cruelty, but she suffered, nevertheless. Her lack of success with the majority of her students and the constant barrage of ridicule were demoralizing.

When the day of her retirement finally arrived, Marge was filled with relief. She secreted herself away in her home, emerging only to attend church and buy groceries until Pastor Greg introduced her to Joey. Joey accepted her for who she was. He never judged her. Because of him, she felt free to be herself.

Skipping downstairs in her yoga ninja outfit, Marge caught her second wind. "Ready!" she called. She danced into the kitchen and did a pirouette.

Joey looked up from the newspaper and said, "Marge, that is a wonderful ninja outfit, but… your hair is going to give you away."

She sat down and frowned. "I can't fit a cap over it."

"Why don't you take it down and let me help think up a solution?"

Marge started pulling pins out of her enormous bun and soon had a significant pile of them sitting in front of her. When her unruly locks were finally free, Joey understood why the bun was so imposing. Her thick, curly hair cascaded to her waist. He studied it carefully. It was beautiful but difficult to hide. "I could braid it for you. Then you could tuck the back into your sweater and wear a cap."

"That's a marvelous suggestion! I haven't worn a braid in years."

Marge smiled. "Let me get my brush and some hair bands." She popped up from the table, enthusiasm restored, and charged back up the stairs.

The braiding was a greater undertaking than Joey had surmised. He failed on his first attempt because he began the braid high, and it was too thick to accommodate the cap. Beginning a second time at the nape of her neck, he was amused when she practically purred. The braid was long and thick, and although it made a ridge under her sweater, when Marge pulled the black cap over her head, she was much less conspicuous.

Looking into the mirror, she said, "You are a genius. Are we approaching departure time?"

"Yes. We want to arrive early enough to find a hiding place."

"Ok. Let us proceed. I've never been to the milk plant before. Have you?" Marge locked the front door as they left.

"I have… some years ago. When I first moved here and was looking for a house, Reginald thought I might be persuaded to invest. He took me out to eat several times and invited me to take a tour of the plant. I found it difficult to extricate myself, and when I did, he was visibly angry, and his charm vanished. He hasn't spoken to me since."

"Poor Reginald. He has been bestowed with so many blessings, but he's never satisfied."

Joey nodded silently, thinking back to the uncomfortable situation he found himself in. *I hope James's meeting doesn't require confrontation with Reginald. That could be very unpleasant.*

Walking through their quiet, darkened neighborhood felt alien. The mostly disused trail through the woods at the end of their street was even darker, thick limbs blocking weak moonlight. Joey felt Marge move closer and handed her his powerful flashlight.

"You'll be able to hold it steadier since your hands are free."

"I don't care for this trail at night. It feels spooky."

"We'll be there soon. If we had gone the other way, it would have taken us twice the time."

Marge shivered.

When the plant appeared before them, it too appeared ghostly in the moonlight. The large, rectangular building with a dozen closed docks where trucks backed in for loading and unloading appeared vacant. Joey asked Marge for the flashlight and extinguished it as they crossed a large parking lot to a single door. Four steps led to the employee entrance, which required an ID badge to unlock. Joey pulled out the badge and opened the door.

"Where did you get that?"

"James gave it to me," he whispered. "He also said he would disable the cameras."

Marge frowned. "Are you sure this is a good idea?"

Joey shrugged and glanced around before motioning her to follow him into the dark building.

Goosebumps prickled her arms. The factory was pitch black, except for small exit lights high above the doors, which made the areas in between appear even darker. The eerie silence was broken by quiet footsteps somewhere on the plant floor to their right. Marge followed Joey along the perimeter wall to an open office door. He stopped abruptly and pulled out a small pen light, shining it on the floor in front of him.

Marge leaned forward and inhaled sharply. "Has he left this earthly plane?"

"I don't know." Joey backed his walker up and knelt to check Reginald's pulse. "Yes, he's dead, but the body is still warm. We need to find out who else is here." He stood, swapped his penlight for the larger one, and, utilizing the wheels on his walker, raced into the heart of the plant.

Fearing for his safety, Marge followed him and the shaft of light from his flashlight with quaking knees, sounding like a motorboat. *Pfft, pfft, pfft, pfft, pfft.* She felt her pulse thumping in her chest and gasped when she ran into Joey, who had stopped.

His flashlight trained on James, lying unconscious between two of the enormous pieces of equipment where yogurt and sour cream were packaged, Joey knelt and felt for a pulse. "He's alive but unconscious. Someone else must be nearby," he whispered. Using his walker for leverage, he regained his feet and continued forward to a large tank with its portal-like door standing open. Shining his flashlight inside, he said, "I wonder why it's open. It looks empty."

"I'll check," Marge said, climbing inside.

"Get out of there!" Joey stage-whispered, horrified.

"How interesting," Marge's voice echoed from inside the empty tank.

Joey had set his walker aside and leaned in to help her out when two hands shoved him forward, pushed his legs inside, and slammed the door. He and Marge sat in inky darkness. "Marge?"

"I'm here. Where's your flashlight?"

"I dropped it when whoever that was pushed me in here." He paused. "Marge?"

"Yes?"

"I don't want to freak you out, but dark, enclosed spaces are huge triggers for me."

"Well, there's plenty of room, and if you close your eyes, you won't see the darkness. Come sit by me and close your eyes. Someone will find us soon."

Joey fought to keep his breathing even and scooted toward Marge's voice. When he touched her arm, she helped him lay his head in her lap and began humming. "Are your eyes closed?"

"Yes." His voice wavered.

"The acoustics in here are amazing. We should sing. What's your favorite song?"

"How about *Bohemian Rhapsody?* I know most of the words to that one."

They began quietly, tentatively, but once they heard the full sound of the echo, their voices grew, bouncing off the walls and surrounding them.

"See? Even better than the shower," Marge said. "What should we sing next? How about *Blessed Assurance?*"

Joey sat up with his eyes closed and continued to sing. They didn't know all the verses, but between the two of them, they sang most of the words and hummed the rest. Joey finally fell asleep mid-song. They both jolted awake to loud rumbling and whirring. The tank rattled and shook, the sound deafening. The noise and motion were terrifying, but when a glop of something cold, wet, and strawberry scented landed on their heads, Marge shouted, "We need to get out of here!" She began banging on the side of the tank and hollering. "Help me out, Joey." More goop fell on their heads, and Joey began to panic again.

They banged until their fists were bruised and then added their feet. "Help! We're in here," Marge yelled. Joey was beginning to hyperventilate when he heard clanking outside, and the door began to swing open.

Chapter 16

Oliver Drake stood at the opening of the tank and gawked. "How did you two get locked in there? And did someone have an accident?" He fanned his nose.

Joey shook his head as he climbed out of the vat and scanned the area. "Long story. Has anything out of the ordinary happened this morning?"

Oliver stared at Joey. "A cat stood in front of this tank with something shiny in its mouth. I kept removing it from the plant floor, but it kept coming back. I guess it knew you were in there."

"Cats have extremely good hearing," Marge said, climbing out behind Joey. Where is the cat now? And where is Joey's walker?"

Oliver glanced around and shrugged.

"No dead bodies?" Joey asked.

"Perhaps I should call the police," Oliver said, eyes wide.

"I'll call Peter. My cell phone didn't work inside the tank. Have you looked in the office?"

Oliver shook his head and led the way. Joey leaned on Marge's shoulder, and Marge called Peter. Flipping light switches as they went, Oliver stopped suddenly when he saw Reginald's body in the office doorway.

"We found him earlier," Joey said.

"Why were you here?"

"Let's wait for Peter, so we only have to go over it once. Can you let him in?" Joey was still leaning heavily on Marge.

"Yes. You come too."

Marge glared at him. "Perhaps you wouldn't mind assisting since we haven't located Joey's walker."

"Of course. I'm sorry."

"Are the other employees here?"

"The morning shift will be arriving in about an hour. I was prepping for the morning run. There's that cat!"

"Fluster!" Marge cried. "What do you have there?" He approached her and laid his treasure on the floor near her feet. "Such a good boy!" She made sure Joey was steady, then bent down to give Fluster a pet, picking up the shiny object he had been carrying and studying it carefully.

Oliver left them standing outside the office and went to let Peter in. He pulled the door open and stood motionless, at a loss for what to say.

"Hello, Mr., um…"

"Drake. Oliver Drake. I believe Ms. Bumfuzzle called you?"

"Yes. I remember you from the Ferris wheel incident. Aunt Marge said there's been a murder."

"Er, yes, possibly. Mr. Beaumonde is dead. Right this way." Oliver turned and led Peter to the office.

Peter checked for a pulse and scanned the office before pulling out his notebook. "Let's start at the beginning."

"You start." Marge elbowed Joey.

"Reginald asked James to meet him here at one o'clock, but James was nervous, so he asked me if I could come and witness what was said."

"And, of course, Aunt Marge had to come too."

"Of course." Marge crossed her arms and nodded.

"So, you arrived at one… where's your walker, Joey?"

"I don't know. We'll get to that. We got here a little early."

Oliver scrunched up his eyebrows. "How did you get in?"

Joey described their arrival and their discovery of the body.

"Could you see any indication of the cause of death?"

"No, I didn't see blood or a weapon, but it was dark."

"I need to call this in. Just a moment, please." Peter stepped away and called the chief at home. "Sir, I'm sorry to disturb you so early, but I'm at the milk plant, and Reginald Beaumonde has been found dead."

"I don't know, sir. It could be murder. I am speaking with the people who found him."

"Thank you, sir. That would be very helpful."

The chief hung up on him after offering to call the medical examiner and the crime scene techs. Walking back to the forlorn-looking trio, Peter said, "I assume you didn't enter the office, so what happened next?"

"We heard footsteps, and we were here to meet James but hadn't found him, so I took out a bigger flashlight, and we walked toward the machinery. He was lying unconscious between those two machines." Joey pointed to the location. "He had blood on his head, but his breathing and pulse were strong."

"The door to that big tank was open," Marge indicated, "so we went to investigate. They are much bigger than they appear. I climbed in to…"

"You climbed in?" Oliver shouted. "What would possess you to do that?"

"I don't know. It was open. I was curious." She shrugged.

"I told her to get out, but she wanted me to lean in so I could see. I leaned in, and someone shoved me the rest of the way in and locked the door." Joey's voice wavered. "We fell asleep at some point and woke up when the tank started making a lot of noise, and yogurt began dripping on our heads."

"I heard banging and voices, so I stopped the machines and opened the door. And there was the cat, too." Oliver wrinkled his nose.

"What cat?" Peter asked.

"Fluster was advocating for our release. He brought us a clue." Marge held up a shiny bracelet. "And when we got out of the tank, Joey's walker was gone."

"And you?" Peter turned to Oliver. "Did you see anything unusual when you arrived?"

"Just the cat." He shook his head.

"Let me see if I have this straight. Aunt Marge and Joey, you discovered Reginald's body and then found James unconscious, then someone locked you in the yogurt tank. Joey's walker and James are now missing. Oliver, you found Fluster, who led you to Marge and Joey's location; when you released them, they took you to Reginald's body in the office."

"Sounds about right," Joey said.

"We need to find James." Peter closed his notebook. "And you'll need to close the factory today."

"Fine by me. The boss won't mind." Oliver frowned.

Peter looked toward the entrance. "We should let the crime scene techs in. Aunt Marge, I think you and Joey can go home now, but I'll want to talk to you again later."

"It's a long way without my walker."

"Do you have a spare at home?"

"Yes."

"I'll find someone to give you a lift, and we'll keep an eye out."

"Thank you, Petey. We'll be at the church later and the potluck after the service."

"That's fine." He nodded and followed Oliver to the door.

Chief Lloyd, the medical examiner, and a squad of techs filed into the plant and began setting up their equipment. Peter summarized the witness statements for the chief and waited patiently for the medical examiner's initial findings. He scanned the scene again, his eyes resting on a plate of cookies on Reginald's desk.

"The time of death was possibly between eleven and one. No visible wounds. He shows signs of hypertensive crisis, but I will need to run some tests before I can make a determination.

Please bag a sample of the emesis and the piece of cookie near his right hand." He stood and scanned the office. "Bring that plate from the desk as well. As soon as you've finished, I'll ride with him to the hospital." Addressing the room at large, the team nevertheless understood, and Peter was relieved that he had noted the cookies.

"Your aunt was present. Again." The chief glared. "She's a murder magnet. Why is she here?"

"James asked Joey to come and…"

"Put it in your report and get her out of here. I have things to do."

Peter decided to give Marge and Joey a ride himself while he waited for the autopsy results. Before he left, he pulled Oliver aside. "Do you know anything about the cookies that were in the office?"

"No, but Georgia would. She knows everything."

"Who's Georgia?"

"Georgia Simon, Reginald's secretary. I can get you her number if you like."

"Yes, please." Peter put the number in his phone and escorted Marge and Joey outside. Silence reigned in the cruiser until Peter pulled into Joey's driveway and got out to help him to the door. "You two try to stay out of trouble until I get back. No more murders today."

"The murders aren't our fault Petey."

His shoulders slumped, and he sighed. "I know. See you later."

Chapter 17

Marge stood with Joey and watched Peter drive away. "Shall we retrieve your walker and prepare our repast?"

"I'd like a nap."

"Me too, but slumber, in my current state, would preclude potluck attendance."

"Okay. We need to talk about what happened anyway. My spare walker is in the hall closet. It's not as good as the new one. I hope they find it."

He unlocked his front door and retrieved his walker from the hall closet. "You meant to make breakfast at your house, right?"

"Of course. Do you even have food in your refrigerator?"

Joey grinned. "I have milk and hotdogs."

Letting themselves out of Joey's house and crossing the street, they found Fluster waiting on Marge's front porch. "We must deliberate certain aspects of last night's events." She bent and picked up Fluster before ushering Joey inside. "You might have rescued us," she told Fluster, "and you must be famished."

"I'll feed him while you make breakfast. We don't want to eat too late, or we won't be hungry later."

"True. How about French toast?"

"Sounds good. I'll make the coffee after I feed his royal highness."

The two quickly made breakfast and sat at the table. Marge had been thinking about that morning's events and began their conversation in the middle of a thought.

"The bracelet is incongruent."

Joey took a bite and raised his eyebrows.

"Maybe we should start at the beginning. What exactly happened last night?"

"Reginald crossed over, and James was wounded before we arrived."

"We don't know that James was wounded before we arrived. Was it murder?"

"Almost certainly. Would you like some more coffee?"

Joey nodded and handed her his cup. "Why are we assuming it was murder?"

"Because he was eating a cookie when he died. Could James have done it?" She filled Joey's cup and handed it back to him.

"I don't think so. Someone else was there, and if they saw him murder Reginald, they would have stayed and called the police. And why would they lock us in the vat?" He gave an involuntary shudder.

"True. How about the hands that pushed you? Did they belong to a man?"

"I don't know. Could we not talk about that part right now?"

"Yes, sorry."

"What were you saying about the bracelet?"

"The bracelet belongs to Elizabeth. She was wearing it in the hospital. What was it doing at the plant?"

"A very good question; however, she could have lost it on a previous visit."

"Food handling requirements are quite vigorous, I believe. James would be a good source of information. Do you have any thoughts on his possible whereabouts?"

"I have no idea where he might be. He's injured, and the police will be looking for him." He glanced at Marge. "We should probably change from our ninja duds to our church clothes."

"What time is it?"

"Eight o'clock. Should we drive?"

"We can walk since you have a basket."

"I'll meet you outside at eight-thirty then."

When Joey rejoined her, Marge was waiting on the sidewalk in front of her house, balancing her coffee cake and trying to adjust her sweater. She handed Joey the cake, which he placed in his walker's basket, then he helped her remove her sweater so she could make another attempt at getting it on straight.

"Would you like some help?" She was flapping around like a bird. "Marge?" Joey helped her get the sweater on and placed his hands on her shoulders. Gazing deep into her eyes, he said, "Tell me what's bothering you." He knew from experience that Marge would react in one of two ways. She chose the pragmatic route, and they began to walk.

"I'm not sure, Joey. Meditation can be helpful when trying to solve a puzzle."

"Do you meditate?"

"Occasionally." She shrugged. "It has a soporific effect."

He turned to hide his smile, then focused his attention on the two churches in the distance, well, the church and the cathedral. Situated across the street from each other, as they drew closer, he could see a steady stream of well-dressed visitors holding containers of varying sizes entering each, but the cathedral was considerably larger and more ornate than the church. "It looks like they're having a potluck as well."

"Hm?" Marge answered distractedly.

"Have you ever been inside Our Lady of Sorrows?"

"I took the children there on a field trip one year."

"It's beautiful inside."

"Yes. We can gain a lot of knowledge through the study of history and art."

Joey shook his head at her convoluted train of thought and greeted the pastor when they reached the top of the steps leading to the entrance. "Good morning, Pastor Greg."

"Good morning, Mr. Cattywampus, Ms. Bumfuzzle." He shook their hands and directed them toward Harriet, who could guide them to the potluck prep area.

"Good morning, Marge. I see you decided to participate this time."

"Of course, dear. Which astonishing masterpiece have you brought today?"

Harriet's cheeks took on a pink hue, and she wiggled slightly as if her tail had been removed. She clasped her hands and leaned toward Marge. "I made traditional haggis," she whispered excitedly.

Marge was dumbfounded. Her mouth formed a small oh. "You'll have to point it out," she said weakly. "Where are the desserts?" Placing her coffee cake with the other sweets, she made wild eyes at Joey.

"You've done your good deed for the month. Where shall we sit?"

"Let's take seats closest to the exit, so visitors are able to get a good view."

Singing hymns together reminded Joey of their hours in the vat. Who but Marge could distract him from a trauma response by singing with him? By the time the sermon started, Joey's eyes had turned glassy. His own efforts at rousing himself were rapidly failing when a loud snort made him jump in his seat. He looked at Marge, head tipped back, mouth open, and elbowed her gently as a long snore began softly, then gradually gathered steam. He kicked her foot and gave her another jab, causing her to jerk upright, eyes wide.

"What did you do that for?"

"Sorry. You were snoring."

Several people around them frowned and said, "Shh!"

Marge pursed her lips and stared straight ahead.

After the service, the congregation relocated to the social hall, where long serving tables were heaped with homemade offerings and round, eight-person tables covered in white cloths salted the thin, brown carpet. Marge transported their heaping plates to Millicent's table and sat with her, wondering how much she had heard about the morning's events.

"I think this is your best souffle yet," Joey declared as he sat and took a bite from the plate Marge handed him.

Millicent stared unseeing. "Thank you," she murmured graciously. "I was told you found Reginald this morning."

"Yes. I'm very sorry for your loss."

"I'm not sure he was a loss, but it was a shock. Elizabeth is taking it very hard." She turned suddenly. "What did you bring, Marge?"

"I brought coffee cake. Would you like me to bring you some? High doses of sugar may be in order this morning."

"Yes, please."

"Joey?"

"Not quite yet, but thank you."

<hr>

Marge approached the dessert table and studied the offerings: fruit, pastries, cakes, muffins, Jell-O salads. Opting for a large plate, she dished out a little of everything. The fruit was particularly appealing. Only half listening, Marge overheard two ladies near her in deep discussion.

"Where's Freida?"

"She's at home looking after James. He showed up at her apartment in the middle of the night with a gash on his head. He refused to go to the hospital."

Freezing mid-scoop, Marge set her plate down and headed for the exit, dialing Peter as she went. When he picked up, she said, "Rumor has it James is at Freida Gottlieb's apartment. Witnessing murder can be precarious to your health."

"Thanks, Aunt Marge. I'm on it."

They disconnected, and Marge stood motionless in the middle of the parking lot. She didn't have the will to go inside, make small talk, or stand in the buffet line. She only wanted to sleep.

Joey's eyes followed Marge through the exit. "Excuse me," he said, rising to follow her. Walking out into the bright sunshine, he shielded his eyes and searched the lot. He approached her motionless form with apprehension. "What are you doing out here?"

"I'm exhausted. Sleep is more alluring than sugar."

"Should I find us a ride?"

"I can walk, but my social skills have deserted me."

"I understand. Let's head home."

Walking along the familiar route, unseeing, Marge tripped twice on the uneven sidewalk before Joey suggested she hang on to the walker. They parted ways to go into their individual homes, but when Joey looked back, Marge had curled up on the porch in front of her door, so he crossed the street and used his key to open it. Coaxing her to her feet, he guided her to the sofa, where she promptly curled up again. Joey brushed her hair back off her face, softened in repose, gazed at her for a moment, then let himself out and went home to get some rest as well.

Chapter 18

Driving directly to Freida Gottlieb's apartment in search of James Nelson, Peter knocked on the door to her apartment on the ground floor of the Belle Estates complex. The white apartments gleamed in the morning light, and potted plants lent them a burst of color. Freida answered the door with a worried frown and, without a word, stepped back to admit Peter.

Lying on the brown leather sofa with an amateurishly bandaged head, James's eyes followed Peter's entrance. "Why did you let him in?"

"You need medical attention."

"I didn't do anything, Sergeant. I swear."

"Did you see who hit you?"

"No," James whispered.

"Let's get you patched up, and then you can tell me what happened, okay?"

"How did you know I was here?"

"You can't keep a secret in this town." Peter shrugged. Assisting James to the cruiser, he drove him to the hospital emergency room and waited while the on-call doctor cleansed his wound and gave him stitches.

"Do you have any idea what kind of weapon could have made that wound?" Peter asked the doctor.

"My best guess would be a heavy, blunt object. The wound is long and narrow, quite deep. You're lucky to be alive, Mr. Nelson. Half an inch in either direction would have proved fatal. As it is, try to rest as much as possible and take ibuprofen for pain."

105

"Thank you, Doctor. Ready to go, James?"

"Yes. Thank you, Doctor."

Leaving the hospital, Peter drove James to the station for questioning, but once they arrived, James refused to say anything until Joey was with him. "I only know part of the story, and Joey promised to be there so he will know more. I need him here to help me fill in the gaps." Peter left a text message for Joey, then telephoned Georgia Simon, Reginald's secretary.

He was surprised by her apartment, which was much more modest than he had expected. He knocked, and after a short wait, a petite young woman with short, blonde hair and big blue eyes opened the door.

"Good morning, Georgia."

"Hello, Peter. Please come in and have a seat."

Peter looked around at the simple furnishings, toys strewn around, and neatly folded laundry. "I assume you've heard about this morning's incident?"

"No, I'm afraid I haven't."

"Reginald Beaumonde passed away this morning in his office."

Georgia gasped and put her head in her hands.

"I'm sorry. I know you were his secretary but were the two of you close?"

"Not particularly. He could be very demanding. It's just… I have a daughter to support, and that job was my livelihood. Will the plant remain open?"

Peter shook his head. "I don't know. May I ask you a few questions?"

She nodded.

"Do you know if he had any appointments yesterday?"

"No, he didn't usually work on Saturdays unless it was an emergency."

"Had he seemed at all different lately? Change of mood, odd behavior, anything?"

"Not really. He might have been a little more… jovial? I don't know if he was happier, but he oozed extra good-ole-boy charm. It was a little annoying."

"Ok. One more question. Did you ever see any strange-looking orange cookies in his office?"

"Yes, but not for quite some time. He wasn't supposed to eat sweets, so his favorite cookies were 'Philly Cheesesteak cookies.' No one else in the plant would touch them. They were disgusting."

"Do you know where he got them?"

"His wife made them. Like I said, he hadn't had any for a long time."

"What was in them?"

Georgia wrinkled her nose. "The main ingredients were cheese and bacon."

Peter stood and extended his hand. "Thank you very much for your time. You've been very helpful."

Georgia stood as well and shook his hand. "You're welcome. Please let me know if you have any further questions." She led him to the door and waved as he drove away.

⬧

After Peter returned to the station, Sally once again arrived bearing coffee. Peter's lips turned up involuntarily. "Thank you! I love it when you visit." He smiled gently. "I don't want to take advantage of your kind gesture, but I have some questions for you regarding Reginald Beaumonde. Part of me doesn't want to intrude on your privacy, but I must."

"It's okay. I know it's your job." She sat down and gazed at him expectantly.

"You know that Reginald died early this morning?"

"Yes, I heard."

"I need to know the nature of your relationship with him."

"There was no relationship."

He raised his eyebrows. "The two of you were seen having a heated discussion behind the cafe."

Sally lowered her head and took a deep breath. "You've probably heard about his affair with my mother."

"What were you arguing about?" Peter asked gently.

"He came complaining to me that Seth punched Carter in the nose, and when I asked him what had led up to that..."

Peter was taken aback by the fire in her eyes.

"Carter is a bully. Seth saw our mom and Reginald making out in the park, then Carter snuck up behind him and gave him a shove, demanding that he stop spying on his dad. Seth saw red and punched him. I found out that Carter has been bullying him into doing bad things and telling him he would get dad fired if he didn't. I was so angry. I told Reginald to keep his dirty deeds away from the festival. What did he expect? He had no shame."

"Yesterday, your father found out that Reginald was the reason your mom left. He must have been angry."

Sally's eyes widened. "Oh, no. Poor dad. I didn't see him yesterday. He didn't... he wouldn't... you don't think *he* did it?"

Peter put his hand on hers. "I don't know, but I needed all the facts."

"Thank you for being kind." She swiped at an errant tear. "I know my family is a complete mess right now."

"I know better than most that we can't choose our families."

"I love Marge. If you ask me, you are lucky."

"She's awesome but largely misunderstood." Peter gave her a sardonic smile.

Chapter 19

Marge called Joey at seven the next morning. "Good morning," she sang. "Want some breakfast?"

"I'll be over in a jiffy." He disconnected, threw on some clothes, and was knocking within ten minutes.

"That was quick. You must be rapacious."

"We missed two meals yesterday. Is it ready?"

"Almost. Have a seat, and I'll bring you some coffee." She was dishing out breakfast when the doorbell rang, so Joey answered the door.

"Good timing," she said as he and Peter entered the kitchen.

Once they were both seated, Marge handed them each a plate and a cup of coffee before sitting with her own.

"What's different about you?" Peter canted his head slightly, examining her. "Your hair! You almost look like a different person."

Marge patted her head and made a face when she felt the dried yogurt. "Joey did it so I could wear a black cap. I had completely forgotten."

"I like it."

"Thank you. I haven't seen it yet, but I'll take that into consideration when I do." She smiled. "So, what's the big emergency?"

"I went to pick up James and took him to the hospital, then to the station for questioning. How did you know he was at Freida's?"

"I overheard two women conversing in the dessert line."

"He refuses to talk until Joey is there. Can you come to the station with me after breakfast?"

"Yes. Marge should come too."

"Why?"

"She was there with me and might have seen something I didn't notice."

Peter sighed and chomped on a piece of bacon. Ignoring him, Marge asked about the autopsy results.

"The autopsy is interesting. Death occurred shortly before you arrived. His stomach contents showed he had been eating the cookies that were sitting on his desk. They contained MAOI medication and large quantities of cheese. Additionally, Mr. Beaumonde had high blood pressure."

Marge summarized. "He suffered from chronic high blood pressure, he was anxious about his appointment with James, and he consumed cookies containing ingredients known to make blood pressure soar."

The three of them sat in silence, pondering the implications.

"Where did he get the cookies?" Joey asked.

"His secretary said Elizabeth made them."

"This time, or usually?"

"Millicent was obliged to acquire cheese a second time."

"And Fluster found her bracelet in the milk plant," Joey added. "We should speak with James."

"Please allow me to tidy up the kitchen prior to our departure." Peter and Joey gave her a hand, then the trio rode to the station in Peter's cruiser.

Parking in front of the entrance, Peter led the way inside to be greeted by his scowling chief.

"Could I speak with you privately, Sergeant Locke?"

"Yes, sir." Peter followed him into a nearby office and shut the door.

"May I ask why you have brought those two crackpots to your place of employment when I specifically asked you not to?"

"I brought them at our witness' request. He refused to speak until they were present."

"Our witness? The suspect you mean. James Nelson?"

"I have new information that points to another suspect. We need his statement."

"You'd better be right," the chief growled. He threw open the door to the office and stomped down the hall.

Peter collected Joey and Marge and led them to an interview room. After procuring an additional chair, he asked a deputy to escort James to the room.

———··◆··———

Despite his size, the dark circles under his eyes and the bandaging on his head made him look frail and unwell, but James smiled with relief when he saw Joey at the table.

"It's time we compare notes and figure out what happened at the plant," Joey said. "Are you up for it?"

"Where should I begin?"

Joey glanced at Peter, who said, "Go ahead. I'll ask for clarification if needed."

"You told me to be at the plant at one, so Marge and I arrived at twelve-fifty. What time did you get there?"

"I might have gotten there about five minutes before you did. I heard you enter. But someone else was there too. I could hear their footsteps. The plant was very dark, and I was standing still, trying to figure out where the other person was, then my head felt like it exploded."

"Do you remember anything before you were attacked? Any impressions?"

"I didn't see the other person at all. It was that dark. But I smelled something, a weird lemony smell. I noticed because it wasn't anything I associated with the plant."

Marge glanced quickly at Joey.

"What happened when you regained consciousness?" Joey asked.

"I was laying on the cold floor, and when I tried to sit up, I felt like my head was on fire. The plant was very quiet, and I didn't know how much time had passed or if anyone was still there. I was afraid." James hung his head, and his shoulders slumped. "What happened to you?"

"We found Reginald's body, and we saw you laying on the floor. I checked your breathing and your pulse then Marge saw an open vat, so we went to investigate. Someone, the killer, I presume, pushed us in and locked the door."

"Wait. Killer? Someone killed Mr. Beaumonde?"

Peter, Joey, and Marge all stared at him.

"What?"

"There must have been a failure in the gossip chain," Joey said. "Why did you think Peter brought you here?"

"I don't know. I guess I thought something must have been stolen or something. All I know is I showed up for a meeting and got ambushed. You were locked in the vat when I came to?"

"That's probably a safe assumption. Did you go straight to Freida's apartment after you left the plant?"

"No. She's been mad at me. I wandered around for a while. I went by your house, but all the lights were out. I was cold and hungry and had shooting pain in my head, but nothing was open at that hour. Finally, I decided I had to take a chance and went to see her. How did the police know where to find me?"

"Marge heard some ladies talking about it at the church potluck."

"It was for the best. The doctor said I had a concussion and needed stitches. He said another couple of inches in either direction would have killed me."

"I asked the doctor about the weapon," Peter said. "He said something heavy and square. Do you remember what was sitting on the wall shelf in the office?"

James looked at Peter uncomprehendingly.

"Something was missing from the shelf. The dust had been disturbed."

James blinked. "Was the safety trophy there?"

"I don't think so. I don't remember a trophy."

"It was shaped kind of like a dumbbell, a long handle in the middle with a thick square on each end."

"We are currently looking for the trophy and Joey's walker."

"I have a question, James." They all looked at Marge. "Did Reginald ever work late at night?"

"I never saw him at night."

"So how did the murderer know he would be there? Did you tell anyone?"

"Just Joey and Freida. She might have told Sally. They tell each other everything." He rolled his eyes. "Do I have to stay here?"

Joey leaned in. "I think it would be wise. The murderer didn't want any witnesses, and he probably thought he killed you. You're safe here."

"What about you?"

"Good point," Peter said. "You could be in danger too."

Marge stood. "I think we should visit Millicent straightaway."

Peter knocked on the door and had James returned to his cell. Once he left, Peter turned to Marge. "I know you are trying to be helpful, and I thank you both for coming here today, but the chief has asked that you not be involved in the investigation. James and Oliver were both at the factory, and they both had a motive. Since James was injured, Oliver is now our prime suspect." Marge opened her mouth to speak, but Peter cut her off. "Let me do my job, Aunt Marge. Will you need a ride home?"

"No, thank you." She pursed her lips.

<hr>

Returning to his cruiser, Peter turned on his siren for the short drive and screeched to a halt in front of the Drake home.

He strode up the front steps and rang the bell, surprised when it was answered by a teenage boy.

"Hello, is your father home?"

"No, I think he's at work."

"Thank you." Peter turned to leave, then stopped. Looking back at the boy, he said, "If you see him, could you ask him to call me. Peter Locke."

"I will, Officer."

Peter drove to the milk plant and knocked on the employee door. As the plant equipment was deafening, no one heard him, so he dialed the office number.

"Beaumonde Milk Plant," said the female voice on the line.

"Georgia? This is Sergeant Locke. I'm at the employee entrance. Could you let me in, please?"

"I'll be there in a minute."

She opened the door with a young child attached to her skirt.

"Hello," Peter stooped to greet the child. "Is this your daughter?" He asked Georgia.

"Yes. Reginald often let me bring her to the office. Come on back."

"I need to speak with Oliver Drake."

"Mama said Uncle Reggie died."

"Yes, I'm afraid he did."

When they entered the office, the child said, "I liked Uncle Reggie. He gave me candy."

Georgia squinted at her daughter. "I told him not to do that."

"Sometimes he gave me other things if I did favors for him."

"What kind of favors?"

"He said not to tell."

Georgia squatted down next to her daughter's chair. "Missy, Uncle Reggie died, and we have to find out why. What kind of things did he ask you to do?"

"Well, one time he gave me a basket of bacon and told me to put it on a bunch of tables in the park – like flower petals at a wedding, he said."

"Did he ask you to do that with nuts on the stage?" Peter asked.

Missy nodded.

"And what did he give you in return?"

"He gave me a scooter."

Georgia got up and paced. "I just can't believe it."

"What's the matter, mama? Did I do something wrong?"

"No, dear, but next time someone makes you a deal like that, please tell me, okay?"

"Yes, mama. Can I draw now?"

Georgia gave her daughter some drawing materials. "I'm going to take a little walk with the policeman now. Please don't leave the office."

Missy nodded distractedly as she began to draw.

Chapter 20

Handing Peter a hard hat and leading him through one of the rolling doors that led to the cooler, Georgia flagged down Oliver as he sped by on a forklift. He lifted a finger and continued down a row of industrial shelving, expertly maneuvering the forklift to slide an enormous pallet of yogurt into a narrow opening three stories high. He then returned and jumped out to greet Peter.

"Is the plant operational again?"

"No, we're required to go through a rigorous disinfecting process before we are cleared. I'm just moving the finished product and sending it out. We don't want it to sit here and expire."

"Who will be taking the helm?"

"I don't know. They haven't told us yet, but we've been instructed to continue operations.

"I'd like you to accompany me to the station. Is there someone who can cover for you while you're gone?"

"No, but the workers know what to do. Could you keep an eye on things until I get back, Georgia?"

"I'll try. Can I call you if we have an emergency?"

Oliver looked at Peter.

"I'll keep you informed," Peter said before leading Oliver to his cruiser.

They rode silently to the station and walked together into the interview room.

Sitting across from each other at the small, white table, Oliver said, "This seems a little déjà vu."

Peter didn't smile. "Do you have an alibi for between eleven and one on the night of the murder?"

"I don't know if it's an alibi, but I was at home asleep until I got up for work at three."

"Can anyone verify that?"

"Again, I don't know. My kids were home, but I don't know if they were awake. Their names are –"

"I know their names. I also know that you had a very good motive for wanting Reginald dead."

Oliver did a good impression of a fish, mouth opening and closing several times. "You think I killed him?"

"You had motive and opportunity. Did you know about his medical condition?"

"No, I don't think so. What medical condition?"

"Did you make the cookies?"

"I don't cook. Sally does all the cooking now that her mom is gone."

Peter stood. "How can you put so much pressure on her? She's working full time and having to do everything around the house. Shouldn't you be helping?"

Oliver stared at him with round eyes. "Are you accusing me of murder or criticizing my parenting skills?"

"Both." Peter shrugged. "Neither. I don't know. What can you tell me about that morning?"

"Look. I know all this has been grossly unfair to Sally. She quit community college to come home and help, and she's the only reason I've been able to carry on." He slumped in defeat. "As far as the murder goes, I didn't like Reginald; he was a degenerate slimeball, but I didn't kill him. I *did* start sending out resumes. When I got to the factory, I went through my usual routine, but that cat kept sitting in front of the one vat. Animals are a huge health violation, and I was worried we were going to have to re-sanitize everything. Little did I know it was much worse than just one cat. I was shocked when I heard banging inside the vat and dumbfounded when I opened the door and found Ms. Bumfuzzle and Mr. Cattywampus inside."

"Why should I believe you?"

"How would I have known that Reginald would be there in the middle of the night? That was completely out of character. And how would I know how to make those disgusting cookies? And why would I let your aunt out of the vat if I was the one who locked her in there?"

Peter thought that over and decided he was right. "Okay. I'll give you a ride back to the plant, but don't leave town."

After Peter had rudely dismissed them, Marge and Joey left the station and watched Peter turn on his siren to drive the five blocks to the Drake home.

"Why didn't you let him give us a ride?" Joey complained.

"We can use the exercise, and besides, the Fireside is on the way."

Joey was soothed by the thought of lunch and allowed himself to enjoy the sunny day. Winter was on its way, along with a host of aches and pains. *I should remember to be grateful.* "Marge? We should come up with a way to keep fit during the winter without traipsing around in the snow."

She opened her mouth, but before she could speak, he said, "I know you love the snow, but aren't there days when you would rather not brave the freezing weather?"

"Perhaps you have a point. I realize the cold causes you discomfort."

Marge automatically reached for the door to the Fireside café at the same time Harriet gave it a violent shove from inside. It swung forcefully, knocking Marge off her feet. Rather than apologize, the red-faced Harriet stepped over her and fled down the street toward her house. Sally rushed outside as Marge and Joey stared after Harriet. "I'm so sorry, Ms. Bumfuzzle. Are you injured?"

"I'm not certain, but perhaps you could lend me a hand."

Once Marge was back on her feet, they entered the cafe, and she scanned the establishment, searching for the cause of Harriet's discomfiture. She allowed Sally to help her to a booth in the corner and ordered a whiskey neat. "Don't judge," she told Joey, who had ordered one as well. "Today it's medicinal."

"Are you hurt?" Joey asked with concern.

"Just bruised, I believe. All of my body parts seem functional. Have you deduced the source of Harriet's ire?"

Joey nodded. "I wonder who she is."

Pastor Greg was sitting at a romantic window seat with an angelic-looking young woman, holding her hands in his and staring into her eyes with adoration.

Marge observed the couple with a furrowed brow. "Surely, he wasn't oblivious to Harriet's feelings. He could have supposed her reaction?"

"He doesn't look like he's noticing anything other than his date at the moment."

Sally arrived at their table with their drinks and said, "The special today is lasagna with salad and French bread."

"Sounds perfect."

"I'll have that, too," Marge said.

"You two are always so easy." Sally smiled. She left to place their order, then walked over to Greg's table with his bill.

Greg accepted the bill, then stood and helped his date with her sweater before heading for the register. Spotting Marge and Joey, he stopped at their table and said, "Good afternoon, Ms. Bumfuzzle, Mr. Cattywampus, I'd like to introduce you to Angelica. We have recently reconnected after years apart. Angelica, these are two of my favorite parishioners. I'm sure you will grow to love them as much as I do."

"Nice to meet you." Her voice was strong and soothing.

Marge smiled. "It's very nice to meet you too." *What a perfect name for her.*

"How do you do?" Joey added. "Welcome to Buckwood."

"I hope you'll be at Bible study on Thursday," Greg said with a smile and a little wave.

"Oh, boy. Turmoil ahead." Joey muttered.

"I just hope Harriet doesn't keep knocking me over. Look. Here comes dinner." Marge put her napkin on her lap and picked up her fork.

"Would you like me to time you?" Sally grinned.

"That depends. Is there a prize?"

"You take your time, and I'll throw in a free piece of pie."

Marge was already eating.

"Where'd you get that appetite, Marge?"

"It must be the frustration. Sometimes Peter can be so obtuse."

"He was certainly adamant about his suspect."

Sally returned to their table, and they ordered a second glass of whiskey.

After she left, Joey asked, "What are we celebrating, Marge?"

She shrugged and shook her head. "I'm sore and upset, baffled, afraid. I don't know what to do, so I'm drowning my indecision in food and drink. Just about the time I figure it all out, I'll need a nap."

Joey chuckled and gave her hand a pat. "We'll walk it off on the way home, and you'll be ready to lead the charge. Otherwise, if we don't figure it out tonight, you can have a bubble bath and a restful sleep."

"Bubble bath… I think I feel a deep clean coming on."

Joey was alarmed. "No, Marge. You need some rest." Marge's deep cleans took days. He had often found her scrubbing the moulding with a toothbrush and on a ladder, washing light fixtures with Windex. She dismantled her refrigerator and dusted the ceiling fans. He firmly believed that now was not the time for deep cleaning. "We could play Scrabble."

"Perhaps. Let's finish dinner and see how we feel when we get home." She continued eating until her plate was bare, then accepted a piece of apple pie a la mode.

"Aren't you stuffed?"

"Yes. I am as full as a pirate's treasure chest. One more whiskey, please."

Joey stared at her. *What?* "Make that two, Sally." Marge didn't appear inebriated, but three was unprecedented.

"I am very disturbed, Joey, and tonight I will celebrate life."

"Where you go, I will follow, mien capitan." He lifted his glass and took a sip.

Marge grinned at him. "We may be sorry tomorrow."

"If you're sorry, I might as well join you."

❧

Exiting the Fireside Café, Joey linked arms with Marge inside his walker and wove unsteadily toward home. They revisited the night before, singing some of their favorite tunes loudly and slightly off-key. Stumbling into Marge's living room, they frightened Fluster, who hid under one of the recliners. Marge walked through the kitchen and out onto the patio, switching on the twinkle lights and placing her favorite record from 'The Great Band Era' box set on her modern record player. *You Go To My Head* began to play, and Marge stood on the deck and swayed to the ballad until Joey approached and asked her to dance. They stood with her right hand in his left and swayed lightly to the smooth ballad, then picked up the tempo when *Flat Foot Floogie* began to play.

Marge laughed and did a somewhat liberal interpretation of the Charleston. "I can remember, as a child, dancing around the living room with a pillow while this was playing. Such wonderful, carefree days."

I wish my childhood memories were as happy as hers. Joey listened to Marge recount her memories and enjoyed them with her. He held her close while they listened to *I Double Dare You*, a song that was already old when they were young.

Marge dozed off while they were dancing, suddenly jerking her head up off his shoulder, wide-eyed. "I think we should call it a night, or I'll be sleeping on the porch."

"I'm starting to fade as well." Joey looked at his watch, startled that it was only five o'clock. "It's still early, though. Maybe we should have some water and left-over pizza. We'll sleep better and maybe prevent a nasty hangover."

"Not a bad idea if I can keep my eyes open. We could try a round of Scrabble while we eat. Would you like me to heat the pizza?" *Didn't we just eat?*

"I like it cold," Joey said from the game cupboard in the living room. "Found it!" he called.

The food, water, and mental stimulation revived them, and they were debating a second game when the doorbell rang. Marge answered the door and took a step back. Standing before her on the front porch was the last person she expected to see. Millicent stood like a soldier, holding a small valise.

Chapter 21

Marge found herself momentarily speechless but soon recovered. "Millicent. Did you walk?"

"Yes. I didn't want anyone to know where I went. May I come in?"

"Of course. Where are my manners? Would you like some refreshments?"

"No, thank you. I stopped at the Fireside on my way here."

"Why don't you have a seat on the sofa and tell me what's troubling you."

Millicent sat, still holding her bag, and for the first time Marge could remember, her shoulders slumped. *That can't be good.* "What happened?"

"Nothing happened exactly. Well, my son and my son-in-law have both been murdered, and Elizabeth was put in the hospital. I'm afraid I could be next. I don't know why, you see. I'm afraid to eat anything at home and afraid to be alone. For some reason, I trust you Marge, and I was wondering if I could stay here until you figure out what's going on."

"You're welcome to stay, but it's the police that are investigating."

Millicent raised her eyebrows and tilted her head. "If you say so, dear. Where is Joey?"

"He's in the kitchen with the Scrabble board. Would you like to play?"

"Yes. That sounds lovely."

"I'll show you to your room first, and you can get comfortable." Marge led the way upstairs to a cozy guestroom.

"You will find additional towels and blankets in the closet and an eclectic selection of books on the shelves. Please make yourself at home. Joey and I will be in the kitchen when you're ready."

"Thank you very much, Marge. I knew I could count on you."

Marge went back downstairs and had a bemused look on her face when she sat across from Joey at the kitchen table.

"What was that all about?"

"Millicent is frightened and asked if she could stay. She'll be down to play Scrabble in a few minutes."

Joey nodded thoughtfully. "I wonder if…"

They both looked up as Millicent entered the kitchen. "Am I interrupting anything?"

"Not at all. Sit wherever you like." Marge began to hand out tiles. "We each draw a tile to see who goes first. Closest to A."

Joey drew C, Millicent drew G, and Marge drew R. "Joey frequently has good fortune."

"I haven't played this game for many years, so I'm not sure how I'll do."

"No worries." Joey laid down 'clues' for ten points.

Millicent laid down 'sage' for seven. "I put sage in the souffle."

Marge put 'shy' for nine.

Joey got a double word for twenty-four when he spelled 'bracelet.'

"Now that's interesting. Fluster brought us a bracelet when we were rescued from the yogurt tank." Marge stood and left the room for a moment, returning with the bracelet. "Look at this, Millicent."

Millicent took the bracelet and examined it. "That belongs to Elizabeth. She said someone stole it."

Marge nodded. "She was wearing it when she was in the hospital."

Handing it back, Millicent laid down 'cheese' on a double word tile and scored twenty-two.

"Did you ever find out what happened to your missing cheese?" Joey asked.

"Elizabeth told me she lent it to someone, but she didn't say who."

Marge spelled 'skims' on a double word tile for twenty-two points. "You said Reginald was running the milk plant into the ground. Did you ever hear rumors about him skimming the profits?"

"I did. Elizabeth told me that, too. I just don't know how much of what she says is true. "

"Joey laid down 'price' and scored thirty with a double letter and triple word."

"You are always so lucky," Marge said.

"It's skill."

"Would either of you like some coffee?" They nodded their assent, so Marge got up to make a pot before returning to the table. The next three words were quiet, jobs, and tornado. "You shouldn't have ended 'tornado' right above the triple word score, Joey."

"I'm just giving you a chance." He winked.

Millicent took the triple word and spelled 'wound' for twenty-seven. "I heard James was hurt the night Reginald died. Did they find the weapon?"

"The police think it might have been the safety trophy from the office. That and my walker are still missing as far as I know."

Marge laid down 'yowl' on a triple letter tile for eighteen. "Just thinking about Fluster's tail. Did the vandals do anything to your house?"

"I don't think so."

Joey spelled 'women' on a triple letter for twelve. "This is getting tough. Shall we invoke the trading policy?"

"After this turn. I have a good one. Your word could refer to Reginald's philandering. I have no idea why he wasn't satisfied at home. He was like a tom cat." Millicent frowned and laid down 'bravery' for twenty. "Marge is very brave."

"Not really." She laid down 'axe' on a triple word for thirty. "I just don't always dwell on possible outcomes before I charge into the fray."

Joey spelled 'vat' for six.

"Why did you have to bring that up?"

"I needed to use my V."

Millicent spelled 'zoo,' and Marge changed 'vat' to 'private for twenty-six. "I wonder if there are more secrets we have yet to uncover."

"Everyone has secrets," Millicent said. "Is that coffee ready yet?"

Marge turned and glanced at the kitchen counter. "It is. Coming right up." She poured three cups and ferried them to the table with the cream and sugar. The next three words were day, teen, and qua.

"Is that a word?"

"It is. I know that because Joey used it before, and I made him look it up."

They started swapping letters and finished the game with pig, egg, fizz (with a blank tile), atone, pi, daft, bin, ail, and loaf. Joey looked at his final letter. "Is 'fi' a word?"

"I don't think so," Marge said, "unless we count 'fee fi fo fum' from Jack and the Beanstalk. One leftover tile isn't bad. Who won?"

"I got 123, Millicent had 151, and you got 197. How did that happen? Have you been secretly practicing?"

"Millicent must be my lucky charm." Marge smiled. "It's getting late. Do you suppose we should get some sleep?"

"We just drank coffee," Joey complained.

"Not really. I made decaf." Marge winked.

"I thought it tasted funny."

"You did not. You didn't even notice."

"You're right. I didn't notice. It was pretty good. I'll head for home so you ladies can get your beauty rest. Are we up for yoga in the morning?"

"I think we should. It's been days, and we'll be getting creaky."

"See you then. Goodnight, Millicent."

"Goodnight, Joey."

After he left, Marge said, "Is there anything I can get you before bed? Do you need a toothbrush or a glass of water?"

"No, I have everything I need. Thank you so much for your hospitality."

"Think nothing of it, and please make yourself at home. If you need a book, a snack, a glass of water, just help yourself. I don't watch television, but there is a set in the living room, and it functions, to the best of my knowledge."

Millicent went into the guest bedroom and unpacked her valise. After performing her nightly ablutions, she sat on the edge of the bed, deep in thought. *I should sell that big old house and buy one like this. I've always hated that house. Maybe Elizabeth and the children can get their own place.* She wasn't sure why she felt so afraid at home, but she sensed danger, and she was glad she had swallowed her pride and deigned to impose on Marge. Donning her nightgown and climbing into the warm, comfortable bed, Millicent slept soundly until awakened by the morning sunlight shining through her window.

Surprised by sounds of laughing and grunting, she dressed rapidly and ventured into the hall. The sounds were coming from Marge's bedroom, so she knocked softly to inquire if Marge was alright.

"Come in," Marge sang.

Entering the bedroom, Millicent froze, unsure of what she was witnessing. Marge, wearing a strange, body-hugging outfit, had her hands on the floor and her rather ample bottom in the air. On a chair beside her, her tablet showed Joey in the same position. On one side of the screen, a young woman gave soothing instructions. Marge lowered herself to her knees and sank back in what the instructor called "child's pose."

"I hope I didn't wake you," Marge said as she began lifting her legs behind her, one at a time, grunting with effort. "If you like yoga, you are welcome to join us tomorrow."

"You didn't wake me. I'll just go downstairs and put the coffee on."

"Thank you! We'll be done shortly."

Millicent noticed Marge's bed was made, and her cat was winding himself around her ankles, trying to get her attention. She quietly backed out of the room and went downstairs. *The things you don't know about people unless you live with them… or across the street, apparently.* Entering the kitchen, she looked around. *Where would I keep the coffee and filters?* She began pulling out drawers and opening cupboards until she found them in a corner cupboard between the coffee pot and the stove.

By the time it was ready, Marge arrived dressed for the day, her long, curly hair still wet from her shower. "Will eggs and bacon be satisfactory?"

"That sounds lovely."

⎯⎯⎯⎯⎯•·⟨∞⟩·•⎯⎯⎯⎯⎯

Marge started the bacon and retrieved a carton of eggs. Whisking the eggs with a fork before adding green onions, salt and pepper, and a splash of milk, she poured a little olive oil in the pan and shredded some cheddar cheese on a plate. She turned the bacon and poured the egg mixture into a second pan. Placing two slices of bread in the toaster, she tilted her head when someone knocked on the front door. "That will be Joey." She smiled.

Wandering into the kitchen and pulling the cat food out of the pantry, Joey said, "Good morning," and gave Fluster a scoop of food. "I see you ladies already have the coffee brewed. Is there anything I can help with?"

"No, you and Millicent can have a seat; this is about ready." Marge dished out breakfast and slid two more slices of bread into the toaster. She poured coffee and took it to the table while she waited for the toast.

"Is this your regular morning routine?" Millicent asked.

"Almost always," Joey said. "We got off track with the festival and the midnight visit to the milk plant. What are our plans today?"

"I don't know. I feel like we should visit Harriet."

"We should check on Mr. Peterson too. And I wanted to check out a new Aikido school."

"Aikido involves a lot of tumbling, doesn't it? Are we flexible enough for that?"

"We can ask."

They both looked at Millicent. "Would you like to come with us? Do you have plans?"

"Would it be alright if I stayed here? I've been so anxious lately; it would be nice to just read or watch television."

"That's fine. Do you have my phone number? You can call if you change your mind."

"I don't think I have it. Could you write it down for me?"

Marge nodded. "As soon as we finish breakfast."

Chapter 22

After breakfast, dishes done, telephone number taped to the fridge, and Marge's bun firmly in place, she and Joey bid adieu to Millicent and stopped outside to debate the wisdom of taking Joey's car. "If we walk, we can stop for a respite at the Fireside on the way to Harriet's. Additionally, if she is there, it will save us a trip."

"You have a point, but it sounds like a lot of walking." Joey frowned.

"We can do it. Where's the Aikido school?"

"It's on the way to the hospital, actually."

"We could stop there on the way and stop at the church on the way back."

"Why the church?"

"Just in case Harriet's there."

Joey didn't have a good argument, so they set off in the direction of the hospital. "Should we call first to make sure he's there?"

"Yes, that's a very sensible suggestion."

Dialing as he walked, Joey asked after Mr. Peterson and made some affirmative noises before hanging up.

"Well? What did they say?"

"He's been moved to a regular room and is accepting visitors. Look, here's the school."

"The sign says closed. Perchance, we can stop in on our return."

Joey nodded.

⁕

Waiting in the lobby to give Joey and Fred some time to talk, Marge saw Elizabeth enter the hospital and check in at the front desk. She watched her but didn't approach. Elizabeth, heaving a great sigh, walked over to Marge and said, "How are you today, Ms. Bumfuzzle?"

"I'm well, thank you. Joey is visiting Mr. Peterson."

"I'm here to get some stitches removed. Have you seen my mother?"

Widening her eyes, Marge fibbed, "No. Is she missing?"

"Probably not. She's forgetful and probably thought she left me a note."

"Perhaps. Could I ask you a question? It's about that cheese your mother bought for her souffle. She said you lent it to someone. Could you tell me who borrowed it?"

Elizabeth looked surprised. "Everyone sure has made a fuss about the cheese. Sally asked for it. She said her mother is gone, and her father doesn't always buy groceries. Oh. Sorry. They're calling my name. Nice to see you, Marge." She hurried toward the desk without looking back.

That was odd. She was almost cordial. Millicent's defection must be really bothering her.

By the time Joey returned to the lobby, Marge was sleeping soundly near a large potted plant in the corner. He almost hated to wake her, but they had additional stops to make, including lunch. "Marge?" He gently shook her shoulder, and her head popped up in surprise.

"Was I sleeping?"

"Yes. Sorry I took so long."

"That's fine. You'll never guess who I ran into."

Marge's story took up most of the walk back to the Aikido school, where a man wearing a hakama met them at the door. He smiled and bowed, turning to lead them inside. "Why is he wearing a skirt?" Marge whispered.

"I don't know. Maybe he'll tell us about that later."

The man in the hakama introduced himself as Nakamura sensei. He was small of stature, with excellent posture, and exuded a powerful, energetic presence. He quietly studied Marge and Joey without judgment. "Tell me why you are interested in Aikido."

"We would like to learn self-defense, but Marge didn't care for Karate."

"Aikido, or the way of peace, is both physical and spiritual training. It can be practiced at any age and level, and we offer several free classes so you can decide if this is appropriate for you."

"We walk and do yoga every day, so we are reasonably fit," Marge told him.

"Excellent. Would you like to sign up for our trial classes to get a feel for the art?"

Joey glanced at Marge, who nodded. "Yes. How often are they held?"

Nakamura sensei handed them each a schedule of classes. "You can choose three classes. I would recommend taking one or two a week when you start to allow your bodies to rest in between."

"Do we need to let you know we're coming, or just show up for the classes we choose?" Joey asked.

"You can just show up, but choose an adult, beginner-level class."

"Thank you." He stood.

Marge stood as well. "Should we wear anything in particular?"

"Just wear something loose and comfortable during your trial period. If you sign up for classes, you will be provided with a gi."

"I'm allergic to natural fibers, so I can only wear synthetic fibers like polyester. Will that be a problem?"

"We'll special order if necessary. I'll look into it for you."

Marge felt grateful for his flexibility and smiled at him. "Thank you, sensei. We will be back soon."

Leaving the school, the two of them were full of enthusiasm as they walked to the church. "Do you think we should start tomorrow?" Joey asked.

"We could. Should we skip yoga so we don't overdo it?"

"Perhaps. We can see how sore we are. Next stop, church?"

"Yes, just in case Harriet is there. How is Mr. Peterson?"

"He's healing. I think my visit did him good. He's already boasting that he'll beat me in our rematch, and he might. How likely am I to get two ringers again? That was a huge stroke of luck."

"You know you can do it, so you no longer have anything to prove."

Joey looked at her and shook his head. "You don't understand."

"Of course I do. I'm trying to encourage you."

Stopping at the church, they were surprised to find the doors to the office and the sanctuary locked. "That's odd. The church is never closed in the afternoon."

"Maybe that's because Harriet was always here to unlock the doors. Let's go get lunch."

"I think we should check on Pastor Greg. This really isn't like him."

Walking around back to the rectory, Joey knocked, then rang the bell. He tried the door and found it unlocked. He stuck his head through the doorway and called, "Pastor Greg? Are you here?"

Marge led the way, searching room to room and calling for Greg. The rectory was a spacious, older home built when large families were not uncommon. The curtains were drawn, and the air was still, giving an impression of disuse. Finally stopping in the doorway to the master bedroom, they found Greg sitting on the floor of the darkened room, unwashed and disheveled. Joey motioned Marge to stay back as he approached the pastor and knelt beside him.

"Greg? What happened? Are you unwell?"

Greg glanced at Marge and clamped his mouth shut.

"Would you like to speak privately?"

Greg nodded morosely, so Joey motioned Marge to leave the room.

"We're alone now. What happened?"

Greg was gaunt and gray in appearance. His eyes were bloodshot and lifeless. He shook his head.

Joey waited.

"Angelica."

"You looked very happy last time I saw you."

"I thought she was a gift from God. She seemed so perfect. I was such a fool. I'm not fit to be your pastor."

"We are all imperfect. That's why God sent his son to redeem us. He can only forgive us if we lay our sins at his feet and ask."

Greg's voice was low and flat. "I have asked, but I can't forgive myself. She professed her love but said she couldn't stay unless she paid her late husband's debts. I lent her money from the church fund, so much money, and then she disappeared. I've let everyone down, and there is no way to pay it back."

"God always has a plan. Let's get you cleaned up and fed; then I want you to get some sleep. We have Bible study tomorrow night. I'll lead the group, but you need to be there. Your flock needs to know that you haven't abandoned them. We'll figure out the rest. Come on, up you go. You have wallowed long enough." He held out a hand to help Greg up, then marshaled him into the bathroom. "I'll have some food ready for you when you get out."

Greg shut the door, and Joey waited until he heard the water running before he joined Marge in the hall. "We need to get him something to eat and to assemble the troops." He led the way to the kitchen and explained the situation as Marge scanned the sorry state of the pantry.

"Let's order something for delivery. His pantry isn't fit for mice," Marge said.

She dialed Harvey at Italian Subs and placed a large order, and when she hung up, she looked at Joey doubtfully. "What should we do about the church fund and his feelings of remorse?"

"If the congregation stands behind him, I'm sure we can come up with fundraisers to replenish some of the money. I will lead the Bible study Thursday evening and talk about love and forgiveness. He needs to know that we don't expect him to be perfect, that he can lead us through failures, as well as triumphs. I'd better go up and check on him. Perhaps I can get him to come downstairs."

The stairs were difficult to navigate with his walker, but Joey managed. Knocking on the bedroom door before entering, he found Greg sitting on the edge of his bed, clean but not visibly recovered.

"Why don't we go downstairs and see what's for dinner?" he suggested.

Greg shook his head. "I don't want to see anyone."

"Come on. Marge is brewing some coffee. We care for you as a friend, and we're not judging you. Let us help."

Greg stood and followed Joey out of the room, his eyes looking suspiciously moist. "Let me carry your walker for you." He took Joey's walker as they went down the stairs, handing it back when they reached the first floor.

Greg and Joey sat at the table, and Marge poured coffee, then went to answer a knock at the door. Returning with two bags full of submarine sandwiches, she said, "Ta-da!" and set them on the table. "I bought all different kinds, so we have all the food groups." She smiled.

Joey cut them in thirds and placed several on a plate before setting it in front of Greg and helping himself.

"It is lunch time," Marge commented. "And we've been doing a lot of walking today. "Would you like another serving, Greg?"

He glanced at his plate in surprise. "Is it gone already? Yes, perhaps another piece or two."

"When was the last time you had water?" Joey asked.

"I don't know."

"I'll get you a glass." Marge stood and searched the cupboards.

After lunch, Joey encouraged the pastor to sleep. "We have an errand to run, but we'll stop by on the way back, and perhaps we can play a board game."

Nodding sadly, Greg slowly mounted the stairs.

Joey stood and watched his progress, then joined Marge in the kitchen.

"What are we going to do about him?" She nodded toward the stairs. "He's a mess."

"Let's call everyone and arrange a meeting, so we can rally support. He needs to know that we care about him."

They divvied up names, and made their calls, then set out in the direction of Harriet's house.

Peter sat at his desk and reread the report he had found there. Responding to a complaint about a parking violation at the milk plant, Officer Frisk impounded a vehicle registered to Elizabeth Beaumonde. Upon inspection of the vehicle, he found a walker and a heavy trophy in the boot. Submitting both items to the lab, he was informed that blood matching that of James Nelson was found on one end of the trophy. There were no fingerprints on the trophy. Peter laid the report on his desk and stood, intending to confer with the captain. Given the recent tension between them, however, he decided to drive directly to the Beaumonde residence instead.

He strode through the station, stopping to witness Elizabeth Beaumonde speaking animatedly with the deputy on duty at the reception desk. Quietly approaching the desk, he said, "May I help you, Mrs. Beaumonde?"

Elizabeth focused her attention on Peter, and the deputy glanced at him with relief evident on his face.

"My mother is missing, and I'm concerned. She's gotten forgetful, and I'm worried something has happened to her."

"Why don't we go into the interview room and talk about it," Peter suggested with a smile, ushering her down the hall. *She has saved me a trip.*

Chapter 23

No longer filled with tourists, the streets of Buckwood were quiet once again. A light breeze blew colorful leaves along the sidewalks, and the green was empty, save one young man throwing a stick for his black Labrador retriever. Gone were the congestion, the rides, and the food carts. Gone were the noisy children, the pigs, and the canopies. Marge was glad. She enjoyed the festival for a few days, but she enjoyed her sleepy little town even more. Joey's voice startled her. "Should we mention this to Harriet?"

"I don't believe that would be beneficial. She must be distraught, Joey. Maybe we can take her a pie, except I don't know what kind she prefers. Do you suppose she made apple because it was her favorite or because she thought it would be undemanding?"

"It must be her favorite, based on her results."

Marge gently opened the door to the Fireside so the bell wouldn't jangle like it did the last time. Holding it for Joey, she caught Sally's eye and smiled.

"Sit anywhere you like. I'll be with you in a moment," Sally called.

They remained at the register. When Sally returned, Marge asked her, "Are you unwell, dear? You don't seem your peppy self."

"We're having some trouble at home. Mother wants to come back, and Dad said no. I understand, but Seth is angry."

"I'm so sorry. Relationships can be difficult, especially when children are involved."

Sally sniffed. "We'll be fine. Somehow. How can I help you?"

"Are you familiar with Harriet's preference in pie?"

"Apple, I think."

"We'll take an apple pie to go, please."

Sally smiled and nodded before returning to the kitchen.

Scanning the restaurant, Joey looked quizzically at Marge. "You don't want to listen in today?"

"Honestly, my brain seems filled to capacity, and I feel exhausted."

"We could postpone our trip to Harriet's house if you need to rest."

Marge smiled at him. "I'm not physically tired. Harriet might need us."

As they waited, snippets of conversation reached Marge's ears.

"The milk plant is going bankrupt."

"Peter Locke arrested Elizabeth Beaumonde."

"Mr. Peterson was shot."

"He's going to be suspended."

"Mrs. Beaumonde is missing. He thinks Elizabeth killed her and hid the body."

Marge shook her head and stared at Joey. "Did you hear that?"

"Hear what?".

"We'll talk about it on the way to Harriet's. Here comes Sally with the pie." Once outside, Marge waited until they had left the town square to relay what she had heard. "Peter has arrested Elizabeth and suspects her of killing her mother. Sometimes I question his deductive reasoning."

"Barring Millicent, haven't all of the clues pointed in her direction?"

"Technically, yes, but due to her pretentions, framing her would have been effortless. We must speak with Peter."

"Now?"

Marge studied Joey's face. "You are not enthusiastic about visiting Harriet, are you?"

"That's one way to put it. I would wait in the proverbial lobby if I could."

"She may rebuff our offer of companionship, but we must endeavor to provide succor."

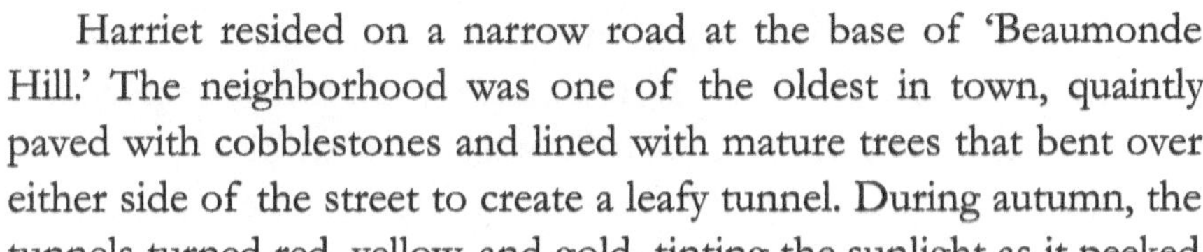

Harriet resided on a narrow road at the base of 'Beaumonde Hill.' The neighborhood was one of the oldest in town, quaintly paved with cobblestones and lined with mature trees that bent over either side of the street to create a leafy tunnel. During autumn, the tunnels turned red, yellow, and gold, tinting the sunlight as it peeked through the branches. Many of the homes were decorated with autumn wreaths and pumpkins, as was Harriet's.

Admiring the house and noting the car parked in the driveway, Marge led the way to the front door and knocked. She received no answer, so she rang the doorbell, hearing the chime within. She glanced at Joey, then knocked once more. "Harriet? Are you home?" she called. "I have an apple pie for you. I'll leave it on the porch." Marge shrugged and set the pie on the porch. She was about to walk away when the door cracked open, and Harriet peeked out with disheveled hair and puffy eyes.

"I'm sorry you walked all the way over here," she said, "but I'm not very good company right now."

"I didn't expect you to be, but I'd love to share a piece of pie and lend a shoulder if you're in need of a friend."

Harriet opened the door wider. "I think I am. Also, if you leave, I'll end up eating that entire pie by myself." Her smile was half-hearted, but it was a start.

"Joey would probably be happier watching television," Marge remarked.

"Doesn't he like pie?"

"He does, but he doesn't like private, female conversation."

"Oh, yes, of course. Why don't you make yourself comfortable in the living room Joey?

The remote is sitting on the arm of the recliner. I'll just see about this pie." Joey wandered off as Harriet pulled a knife out of her kitchen drawer, staring at it momentarily before opening the pie box.

"I asked Sally your preferred pie, and she suggested apple."

"I love apple pie. I even tried to make one for the competition, but you'll remember how that turned out." She frowned. "I wonder if *she* bakes perfect pies." Her face crumpled, and tears threatened.

"Would you like me to do that?" Marge indicated the pie.

"No, I can do it. Why did you go to all this trouble? Walking way over here and bringing pie? I've never been very nice to you."

Marge looked into her eyes and said, "Sometimes friendship is not about what you can get in return. I know you have a good heart, Harriet, and I know you must be hurting. I am here because I care about you."

"And Joey?"

"Joey is here because I made him come with me." Marge laughed.

Harriet smiled a little bigger that time. "Take him some pie, then, and I'll cut some for us."

Marge took Joey his pie, which he happily accepted. Having found a basketball game on the television, he had his feet propped up and Harriet's cat, Willow, sitting on his lap. "Thanks, Marge," he whispered.

She returned to the kitchen to find Harriet sitting at the table with two pieces of pie and two cups of tea. Marge sat with her and took a bite.

"This is way better than mine."

"If you'd like some advice, I would say that you might try cooking the apples a little longer, with just a touch more sugar."

"I ran out of time and sugar. I was so busy trying to be indispensable to Pastor Greg that I didn't have any time leftover for myself. Now, I feel like a fool."

"Was there anything you enjoyed about your duties at the church, anything that didn't depend on Greg's approval?"

Harriet's brow furrowed in thought. "I like planning events and being responsible for things. I liked opening the church every morning, organizing the potluck, being the mc for festival events, but I over-extended myself. Everything became a chore, and it made me cranky. I kept volunteering for more because I thought Greg needed and appreciated me."

"I think he probably does need and appreciate you, just not in a romantic way. He told me that he and his lady friend reconnected after a long time apart. I don't think his feelings are recent; it's possible he has always held a candle for her."

Harriet's eyes widened. "I didn't know that. That makes a difference, doesn't it? He never talked to me about his private life, and he spent all his time at the church, so it didn't occur to me that he might have a long-lost love."

Marge nodded. "The church was locked when we stopped by before lunch. Have there been days when you've opened the sanctuary even though Greg has been absent?"

"No, unless he had a doctor's appointment or was visiting a member of the congregation."

"Who knows? Perhaps he will offer you a paid position as the church secretary once he figures out you are no longer at his beck and call. And Harriet?"

She looked up expectantly.

"You are a lovely and vivacious young-ish woman. Just because one man is unavailable doesn't mean there aren't any out there. I believe Roger is quite taken with you."

"Hey. What do you mean young-ish?"

"Well, you're not in your twenties, but you're a little younger than me." Marge winked at her.

"Watch it, granny, or I'll call the fashion police."

They laughed together and finished their tea.

"Thank you so much for coming, Marge. Thank you for the pie and the conversation and your friendship. I feel so much better."

Marge beamed and gave her a big hug when they stood.

"Joey," Harriet called out, "you get to go home now."

He got up and looked longingly at the television. "Thank you for the pie."

"You can bring more and share it anytime you like." Harriet laughed. "Thank you both for coming over. I'll see you on Sunday."

Chapter 24

Marge and Joey left Harriet in much better spirits and walked back through the colorful leaf tunnels toward the town square. "Let's stop at the grocery store. I'm running low on staples, and it's probably time we had a home-cooked meal other than breakfast."

"Okay. I'll come in too so I can supervise."

"You might want to get a little food to keep in your house. What if I got sick or we got snowed in?"

"Are you trying to get me to eat at home? I would burrow to your front door and cook for you."

"Can you even cook?"

"I can make fried eggs, steaks, potatoes, and spaghetti from a jar. Oh, also toast, canned soup, and frozen dinners. We're set in case of emergency as long as you buy those things."

"Okay, come in and supervise. I definitely don't want you to eat at home."

They entered the supermarket and used the basket on Joey's walker for a cart. Since they didn't often shop together, their expedition was something of an adventure. They discussed the various cuts of meats and bought some items they didn't often have on hand, such as tortillas, soba, and frozen lasagna. Once they had added milk, eggs, fresh fruits, and vegetables, the basket was full.

"Is it difficult pushing the walker with all those groceries in the basket?"

"No, as long as the wheels are out."

"Maybe we should bring the car when we shop."

"I don't mind, but it's been a busy day. That rest at Harriet's house was helpful."

Going through the checkout, they ran into Mrs. Waddle buying canned dog food and treats for Sir Chewalot and gossiping with the checker. "They still haven't caught those vandals, as far as I know. Maybe they were from out of town and left after the festival."

The checker was nodding on autopilot as she scanned the few items, placed them in two bags for easier transport, and took payment. "Thank you, Mrs. Waddle. See you again soon." Turning her attention to Marge and Joey, she began scanning their items and making small talk.

Mrs. Waddle, catching sight of Marge and Joey, stopped to say hello and asked, "Have you heard any news on those vandals?"

"No," Marge said as she handed the checker her debit card. "It is interesting that nothing more has happened since the festival. I'll ask my nephew about it next time I see him."

They walked out together, Mrs. Waddle a constant stream of gossip, which was helpful at times and slightly annoying at others.

Stopping by the rectory as promised, Joey found Pastor Greg sleeping soundly, so he left a note on the kitchen table. By the time they arrived back at Marge's house, they had completely forgotten about Millicent and were alarmed by loud voices coming from inside. Luckily, Mrs. Beaumonde was sound asleep because she might have been surprised when Marge leaped through the front door. Standing in a comical horse stance with her karate-chop arms swinging wildly, she suddenly stopped and dropped her arms.

Millicent opened her eyes and said, "Why are you panting? Did you run home?"

Joey laughed. "We just did some grocery shopping. Are you getting hungry?"

"I hope you don't mind, but I made dinner. I wasn't sure when you would be back."

"We don't mind at all. What did you make?" Marge asked.

"I made salad, meatloaf, mashed potatoes, and carrots."

"That sounds delicious! Is it ready now, or should we put the groceries away first?"

"Let's put them away, so they don't spoil, but it's ready."

<hr>

Millicent served dinner and sat with Marge and Joey at the table. After Joey had tried everything and declared it superb, he addressed the troubling information Marge had overheard at the Fireside Café. "We overheard someone say that Peter has arrested Elizabeth for the murders and accused her of killing you as well. Marge doesn't believe that Elizabeth is guilty, and we know, of course, that she didn't kill you. He told us to stay out of his investigation, but I think we need to ask him here."

Sitting agog, Millicent suddenly started laughing. She laughed so hard she had tears in her eyes. "Poor Elizabeth, so proud and such a snob. This must be the most horrific thing that could possibly happen to her." She wiped her eyes with a napkin. "Of course, you should ask Peter over. You can bribe him with my homemade cherry pie."

"Do you think she could be responsible for the murders?" Marge asked.

"It had crossed my mind. She is very concerned with money and her social standing, but when I really consider her personality in conjunction with the murders, I don't think she could be either that clever or that stupid."

Marge canted her head.

"The murders were very carefully planned, but the killer left clear clues that pointed directly at Elizabeth. She is neither a careful planner nor an idiot. When Peter gets here, we can go through the clues and consider each, but I don't personally think it could be her."

"I'll invite him over." Marge walked into the living room and rang Peter's cell phone.

"I have a suspicion that you'll want to discuss the case, and I've told you that I can't," he said.

"Just come over, Peter. You will be glad you did."

He groused a little more before agreeing to be there within a half hour. Marge disconnected and wandered back into the kitchen, where Joey and Millicent were tackling the dishes.

"He'll be here soon. Should we create a list of clues or wait for him to supply the evidence?" Marge picked up a towel and started helping to dry the dishes.

"Let's wait and see. He might not have even thought of all of them." Joey handed Millicent a pot.

"I don't remember where I found this. Where does it go?"

Marge looked at the steaming basket and pointed to the cupboard where she stored the pans. "On the upper shelf in that cupboard."

⸻ ⟨⟩ ⸻

Peter approached his aunt's door with trepidation. He rang the doorbell and was astonished when Mrs. Beaumonde senior opened the door. Stepping backward, he gaped.

"Good evening. Won't you come in?" she asked.

"H-how long have you been here?"

"Since yesterday evening." She smiled. "Marge heard some interesting gossip in the café today, so we thought maybe we should have a meeting. Would you like to come in the kitchen for some homemade pie?"

"Yes, please," he said quietly.

He followed Millicent into the kitchen and stared at his aunt and Joey, seated at the table with a pie in the middle. *She looks so innocent, but she has me over a barrel, and she knows it.*

"It's good to see you, Peter."

"Good to see you too, Aunt Marge."

"I suppose you are wondering why we asked you to come."

Peter gulped and nodded, accepting a substantial piece of pie.

"We heard some gossip in the café and thought you might like some input."

"You heard about Elizabeth," Peter guessed, assuaging his nerves with a large bite of pie.

"Yes, and Millicent, upon reflection, doesn't believe she is 'clever enough nor stupid enough' to have committed those murders, so we'd like to go over the evidence with you and add any missing information that might lead you to an informed decision."

"What did you mean by that, Mrs. Beaumonde?"

"Doesn't the evidence seem rather obvious? She would have some sense of self-preservation."

"I don't know." Peter shrugged. "The first clue is her perfume, which she bragged to Marge was extremely expensive. Aunt Marge smelled it in the closet, at the hospital, and in the milk plant."

"Elizabeth complained that someone stole her brand-new bottle, still in its packaging, around the time Gavin came to visit."

Peter finished chewing. "Then there's the missing cheese that she needed to make the cookies."

"What did she tell you about the cookies?"

"She said that she hadn't known Reginald was working late, and there's no way she would make him cookies after Sally told her he was having an affair with her mom."

Millicent nodded. "She told me she had given someone the cheese."

"In her statement, she said that Sally told her Reginald had taken her mom away and her dad didn't always buy groceries. Elizabeth felt guilty by association and gave her the package you were saving for your souffle." Peter supplied. "Then there's the bracelet."

"Again, Elizabeth claimed that it was lost or stolen, so the murderer could have seen it lying around and thrown it into the mix to confuse things."

"The final nail was finding Joey's walker and the trophy from the office in the boot of her car."

"Why was that a big secret? Were you planning to notify me before I ordered a replacement?" Joey inquired.

"We didn't release the information, but I also haven't seen you since we found it."

"That's really no excuse, and anyone could have put those things in her boot to make her look like the culprit. Where did she park her car?"

Glad he had already finished his pie, Peter looked at the panel of three and suddenly felt inept. They had blown his evidence to smithereens in the time it took to eat dessert. "If Elizabeth isn't the murderer, then who is?"

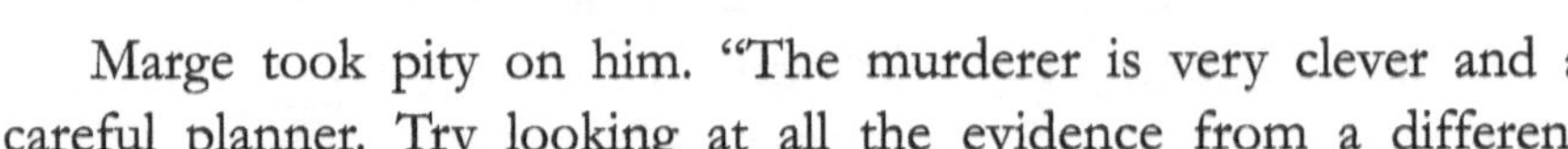

Marge took pity on him. "The murderer is very clever and a careful planner. Try looking at all the evidence from a different perspective, and we'll all get together at Millicent's house Friday evening."

"But that's when I finally have my date with Sally."

"Bring her along," said Millicent with a twinkle in her eye. "We'll make it a party."

"With hors d'oeuvres and champagne." Marge enthused. "It can be Elizabeth's homecoming party."

"She won't appreciate it," Millicent warned.

"That's okay. It's not really for her, anyway. Invite Oliver and James."

They agreed to meet at the Beaumondes' house at seven in the evening, and Peter rose to leave. "May I walk you out, Petey?" Marge walked him to the door and went outside with him. "You might interview Seth and Carter, separately, about the vandalism.

Reginald was the instigator, but Carter was participating and coercing the other boys into helping. If you solicit information from the boys, you can wrap up that case as well."

"Thanks, Aunt Marge. I'm sorry I told you to stay away from the case. I just didn't want the chief angry with me again. He threatened my career."

"I understand, Petey. Could you do me a favor? When you speak with Elizabeth, ask her where she parked her car the night of Reginald's death, and ask her if she had a glass of wine with the man in the closet."

Peter tilted his head and furrowed his brow. "I suppose it can't hurt."

"See you tomorrow." Marge smiled and hugged him before going back inside.

Chapter 25

We need to invite Chief Lloyd, and he doesn't like us," Joey said.

"I'll invite him. He likes our donations. Also, I have a request."
Marge and Joey looked at her.

"I'd like to make a little announcement about my new trust before we begin. I will feel safer if everyone present knows that they won't inherit anything if they kill me."

"That sounds like a very good plan." Joey began clearing the dessert plates. "I assume you have a little idea, Marge."

"I do, but I need to think about it some more. Let's get a good night's sleep. Yoga tomorrow?"

"Absolutely. Millicent?"

"No, I think not. I'll take coffee duty again and put a call through to the chief."

"I'll head home then. See you two in the morning." Joey let himself out and walked across the street.

Peter was off for the night, but he was debating whether he should free Elizabeth or wait and ask her to sit in his interview with Carter in the morning. He also wondered if it would be wise to let the other suspects know she had been released. As long as she was in jail, the murderer thought he was safe. *I should have asked Aunt Marge. She would know what to do.* Sitting in front of the station with his car running, he played out various scenarios in his head, finally deciding to go inside and discuss his dilemma with Elizabeth.

He turned off the ignition and went inside, stopping at the desk for the keys to her cell. His footsteps echoed in the hallway, and Elizabeth was sitting upright on her cot when he got to her cell, inserted the key, and stepped inside.

"Should I hit you over the head and steal your keys?" she asked.

"That would probably just get you locked up again."

"You mean I'm free?"

"Yes, but I wanted to run a couple of things by you first."

She looked at him and blinked.

"I've spoken to your mother, along with Marge and Joey, and they have convinced me that you are not the murderer."

Elizabeth heaved a big sigh. "Thank goodness. I thought everyone had lost their minds."

"That being said, the real murderer thinks he's safe right now. If he finds out you've been released and feels threatened, I don't know what he'll do. I can release you now, but I'd prefer you don't let anyone know. We're having a little welcome home party for you at your house on Friday night, and then you can let people know. Is that acceptable?"

"Yes. It will be nice just to sleep in my own bed and have some privacy."

Peter nodded. "The other thing is that I would like to interview Carter about the vandalism."

Elizabeth's eyes widened, and she was about to launch into a tirade, but Peter stopped her. "I know that he was participating, helping Reginald at least, and bullying some of the other boys into helping. The vandalism has stopped since Reginald's murder, but I would like to wrap up the case with the boys' assistance."

"I suspected Reginald might have been behind my accident. How can I help?"

"I would like you to be present since he's a minor, but I don't want anyone to see you around town. Perhaps I could visit you at home tomorrow morning? What time does Carter leave for school?"

"He leaves around eight. Why don't you come at seven? I'll make sure he's up and ready to talk to you."

"Thank you. Can I give you a ride?"

"Yes, please. Thank you, Peter. I appreciate your thoroughness."

He smiled. "Let's get your things so you can get home."

Up bright and early the next morning, Peter knocked on the Beaumonde door at seven o'clock and was surprised when Elizabeth answered. "Come in. Carter refused to get out of bed when I told him you were coming, but maybe your presence will rouse him." She led him to Carter's bedroom and opened the door. "Just a moment. I'll get you a chair."

Eying the still form in the bed, Peter considered how to approach the subject; Carter had just lost his father, after all. "Good morning, Carter. I'm Sergeant Locke. I'd like to ask you some questions about the vandalism that took place during the festival. I know that you participated to some extent and that you coerced your friends to take part, but I can't imagine you causing your mother's injury."

Elizabeth stood frozen in the doorway with a chair, not wanting to interrupt.

Carter sat straight up in bed and glared at Peter. His dark hair was tousled from sleep, and his eyes wide. "There's no way I would have done that to my mom."

"But you know who did."

"Not for sure, but my dad is the one who gave me ideas. He called them pranks and said when he was my age, he was one of the cool kids. I wanted him to think I was a cool kid too." He shrugged.

"The pranks stopped after the festival."

"Dad was murdered, and I didn't have any ideas of my own. Plus, some of his pranks were getting dangerous. I never wanted to hurt anyone."

"Are you left-handed?"

"Yes. So was dad."

"Thank you for your honesty. I know you have a lot on your plate right now, but we'll have to arrange some community service at a later date to make restitution for property damage."

Nodding solemnly, Carter said, "Thank you, Sergeant. I'm sorry I did those things. Even though they weren't my ideas, no one made me do them."

Peter shook his hand. "I will be in touch. You'd better be getting ready for school." He left the room, and Elizabeth, leaving the chair in the hall, saw him to the door.

"Thank you for your kindness, Peter. I'll see you tomorrow evening."

"That reminds me, where was your car parked the night Reginald was killed?"

"He drove it to the plant because his was in the shop. I didn't know it was gone until I went to retrieve it from the garage. I was going to report it stolen, but the police showed up to notify me of his death, and everything else took a back burner."

"One other thing. Did you have some wine with Gavin the night he died?"

Elizabeth's eyes widened. "How did you know that?"

"It was Aunt Marge's theory. What happened to the bottle and the glasses?"

"I took my glass of wine when I left, but I don't know what happened to the bottle. I didn't know he died, either, and have no idea how he ended up in the closet."

"What did you talk about?"

"I wanted to know what his intentions were, why he had suddenly shown up."

"Did he tell you?"

"He laughed and said that part of the inheritance was his; in fact, as first born, maybe he should inherit everything. He made me angry, so I left."

"What time was that?"

"It was pretty late. One or two in the morning."

"Thank you very much. That should help." He took his leave and headed for his aunt's house.

Waking again to bright sunshine, Millicent took her time getting ready, ignoring the grunts and laughter down the hall. Singing hymns in the shower and styling her hair, she dressed for the day and went downstairs to make coffee. She contemplated making breakfast but didn't want to interfere with Marge's routine, so she sat down and called Chief Lloyd.

His chirpy secretary answered the phone and informed Millicent that he was in a meeting. "Could you do me a very big favor and let him know that he's invited to a small cocktail party Friday evening? Seven o'clock at the Beaumonde estate. He can call Millicent if he has any questions." The secretary assured her that she would give him the message.

Disconnecting with a smile, Millicent noticed Fluster standing by his bowl and staring intently in her direction. "I have been here long enough to know what you want, you rascal." She got up and opened the pantry. The cat food was easy to spot, but she wasn't sure how much to give him. "How much does a cat your size eat?"

"Mrow." Fluster thumped his hairless tail on the floor and stared.

Millicent took a small scoop out of the bag and examined it before filling it and pouring the food in Fluster's bowl. He pushed her hand away and began to eat, dismissing his newest servant once she did his bidding.

Marge entered the kitchen and laughed. "He persuaded you to provide his victuals."

"I didn't know how much I should give him. Is one scoop adequate?"

"Perfect. He will attempt to con Joey into feeding him again. Just wait and see. What would you like for breakfast?"

"I'm not picky. I would have started something, but I didn't know if you had something in mind or have a schedule, so I called the chief and fed the cat."

"Let's have pancakes." Marge poured herself a cup of coffee and began pulling bowls and ingredients from the cupboards.

"Is there anything I can do to help?"

"There's a can of frozen orange juice in the freezer and a pitcher in that cabinet if you'd like to make some. Orange juice sounds good to me this morning."

By the time Joey let himself in, Marge had placed the first stack of pancakes on a plate, adding more batter to the frying pan and placing condiments on the table. "Mmm pancakes," he said.

"Millicent fed Fluster, by the way, so don't let him con you."

"Got it." He sat down at the table and accepted a glass of orange juice. "Do we have plans today?"

"We have to make some preparations for tomorrow evening's party. Anything else?" Marge placed another stack of pancakes on the plate and went to answer a knock at the front door. Opening the door, she found Peter looking like he might burst. "I have information. May I come in?"

"Of course. Would you like some pancakes?"

"Yes, please."

Marge led him into the kitchen and served him a stack of pancakes and a cup of coffee, then waited for him to take a bite before he divulged his information.

"I spoke with Elizabeth last night before I released her."

"Are you sure that was a good idea?"

"I asked her to stay at home until after the party, so word wouldn't get out, but that's not what I wanted to tell you. Elizabeth told me that Reginald drove her car to the plant that night because his was in the shop."

Marge nodded.

"Also, she said that she took a bottle of wine to Gavin's room the night he died because she wanted to talk to him about his intentions. They had an argument, and she stormed out with her glass of wine, leaving the bottle. She said she didn't know he was dead until she got home the next day and had no idea how he got in the closet."

"What happened to the bottle and Gavin's wine glass?" Marge asked.

"I saw a wine bottle and glass in the kitchen but didn't realize they were connected to his death."

"Those were excellent questions, Petey."

Peter smiled and finished his pancakes.

"I was thinking about driving from the plant to the house to time the route, but since Reginald had Elizabeth's car, it won't be necessary. Have you invited James and Oliver to the party?"

"Yes, and I decided not to tell Sally ahead of time because I've waited a long time for this date, and she might cancel. Hopefully, we'll be able to do something of her choosing afterward."

"That sounds like good logic," Joey said. "Maybe take her some flowers, too."

Peter stood and took his plate to the sink. "Thank you for breakfast, Aunt Marge. I have to get back to work."

Chapter 26

Once Peter had left, Marge sat back down at the table and said, "Joey, perhaps Millicent would like to tour the countryside in your magnificent automobile. You could make a detour at the grocery store upon your return. I must ruminate."

Knowing exactly what that meant, Joey readily agreed. Marge was about to embark on the deep clean. "Don't overdo it, okay? We do have plans this evening."

"Just the living room. I promise."

"Let's go for a ride, Millicent. You do *not* want to be here for this."

Millicent followed uncomprehendingly. Standing on the sidewalk as directed, she gazed in awe as Joey backed his beauty out of the garage.

"I bet this car looks better than the day it was made," she said as he helped her into the passenger's seat.

He got in the other side and said, "Thank you. Restoring it has been my pride and joy." He backed out of the driveway and, with one last glance at Marge's house, carefully drove toward the narrow country road that led south, out of town. The sun seemed to light the trees on fire, their golden leaves dazzling against the bright blue sky.

"I rarely come this way unless we're heading for the city. I had forgotten how beautiful it is."

"Marge and I don't drive much at all, but we occasionally drive out here in the winter because she likes to play in the snow."

"You don't?"

Joey smiled. "My old injuries ache in the cold. I get dressed up in long johns and snow pants when we come out, but then need a hot bath and pain medicine afterward."

"You could just refuse."

"No, friendship is a give and take. She loves the snow, and I like to see her happy. It's a small price to pay."

Millicent was quiet for a moment. "Your friendship is a real gift."

"It is. She's my other half. I don't know what I would do without her."

"Why don't you marry her?"

Joey chuckled. "Pastor Greg asked me the same thing, but we don't want to get married. We like having our own space. Is that strange? Would marriage make us better friends?"

"I don't know. I wasn't friends with my husband. It was more like a business arrangement. Isn't there a saying about not fixing what isn't broken?"

"I believe there is." Joey nodded. "Look. There's a pumpkin patch. Would you like to stop and look around before we head back?"

"Yes, let's. We can look in the gift shop and get some hot cider."

<hr>

As soon as Joey and Millicent left on their outing, Marge assembled all her cleaning paraphernalia and began her assault on dirt and disorder. She vigorously washed windows, dusted knick-knacks, moved furniture, and vacuumed as if her life depended on it. The mindless banishing of disorder quieted her mind and allowed her to organize her thoughts, like shuffling a deck of cards. Now and then, she stopped, staring into space.

When she moved the sofa to vacuum, she found one of Fluster's treasures. Gently retrieving the small heart-shaped locket, which hung from a delicate gold chain, she turned it over and read 'love Gavin' on the back.

Inside was a small photo of the happy couple. Marge slid the necklace into her pocket and continued to clean. When Joey and Millicent returned, they found the living room and Marge in complete disarray.

"What happened?"

"This is Marge's form of meditation," Joey explained. "Can I give you a hand, Marge?"

"I have concluded my task, with the exception of returning everything to the proper position." Marge was busy lining figurines along the shelves. She then began righting furniture. "Did you purchase ingredients for the hors d'oeuvres?"

"No, I asked cook to prepare them. All we have to do is show up. Although, you might need a shower, dear. You look like you took on Goliath and won."

"I must admit, I feel a little grimy. Could you and Joey prepare our repast? It needn't be elaborate." Finishing her project, Marge went upstairs to shower while Millicent and Joey took inventory of the pantry.

⁂

Discovering canned tuna and minestrone soup, Millicent set Joey to work chopping green onions, dill pickles, and tomatoes. "I forgot. You don't like pickles, and Marge doesn't like tomatoes. We can keep those on the side." Millicent diced cheese and placed it in a bowl with the tuna, Miracle Whip, and a drop of mustard. She added the green onions and course pepper and mixed thoroughly. Heating the can of soup, slicing apples and pears, buttering the bread, she placed everything on the table with a container of cottage cheese. Joey set the table and started the coffee.

When she entered the kitchen, Marge looked at the table and said, "This is better than the Fireside. Thank you both. Everything looks marvelous."

"I am so grateful for you. I wish I could do more. Have a seat, and we'll eat. You must be starved."

"Putting the pickles and tomatoes on the side was an excellent idea." Marge put the tuna salad on a piece of bread and added a spoonful of pickles.

"It was." Joey added tomatoes to his.

"What do you think about that house that's for sale down the street?"

"We haven't seen the interior, but this is a nice quiet street." Marge took a bite.

Joey drank some soup. "Except it's next door to Mrs. Waddle."

"Is she a difficult neighbor?"

He sipped some more. "She's nice enough. Likes to gossip. But her terrier, Sir Chewalot, is yappy."

"You've been living in a house with no neighbors for many years. Will the noise bother you?" Marge asked.

Millicent nibbled on a piece of fruit, tilting her head to the side and furrowing her brow. "I don't think so. Elizabeth and Reginald argued loudly and often, and the kids have large groups of friends over. It can get downright chaotic. I would like to see that house."

"I'll call the real estate agent after lunch. It would be fun to have you as a neighbor." Marge smiled.

***

Once they had finished lunch, Marge made her call and did the dishes.

"I'd like to take a rest, Marge. Is it okay with you if I meet you back here at six?"

"Of course. We'll view the house and take our repose as well." She thought Joey looked a little out of sorts, so she followed him to the door and said, "Are you feeling indisposed?"

"No…"

"What is it?"

He looked down and mumbled, "I just worry about disrupting our perfect balance."

Walking around so she was partially inside his walker, Marge gave him a big hug. "I won't let anything disrupt the balance. That is of A-number one importance."

"Thank you, Marge, for being my best friend." He hugged her back, then kissed her on the cheek.

"And thank you for being mine." Marge smiled and opened the door for him, waving as he glanced back at her.

Closing the door, she turned to find Millicent in the doorway to the kitchen with her face scrunched. "Am I interfering with your friendship?"

"No, nothing could interfere with that. Joey was just having a moment of doubt." Marge smiled. "Are you ready?"

"Yes, I'm quite excited. How does Joey deal with the stairs?"

"He has an electric chair lift but also converted his family room into a bedroom, so he resides primarily on the ground floor."

"Stairs are becoming increasingly difficult as the years go by."

They left Marge's house and walked down the street, meeting the agent, who was chatting with Mrs. Waddle. Sir Chewalot was barking excitedly and jumping against the picket fence.

Turning and beaming the full force of her sales charm upon Millicent, the agent said, "Hello. I'm Christine. You must be Mrs. Beaumonde." She stuck out her hand.

Millicent dutifully produced a limp hand. "Yes. Thank you for coming."

"How exciting, Mrs. Beaumonde. I hope we'll be neighbors." Mrs. Waddle's voice quivered with sentiment.

Millicent smiled. "Well, let's take a look inside and see what we think."

Christine produced a key and opened the front door. Stepping inside the house, Marge and Millicent froze, speechless.

Chapter 27

The layout of the house was similar to Marge's, but the walls and ceiling were covered in primary-colored, abstract murals. Millicent opened her mouth and then closed it again, prompting Christine to quickly explain that the owner was a local artist. "I recommended repainting," she said, "but he couldn't bear destroying his art."

"It will be difficult to make these walls white again," Marge pointed out.

"Is the whole house like this?" Millicent asked weakly.

"No. Let's look at it and then revisit the living room." Christine led the way into the kitchen.

Millicent sighed in relief when she saw it was pristine, then looked out French doors at a beautiful, blue-tiled swimming pool with a waterfall feature. "How lovely."

Christine smiled. "That is one redeeming feature where his artistry worked to his advantage. Let me show you upstairs."

The stairwell was painted in gaudy colors like the living room, but once they had gained the landing, the walls changed to off-white and the carpet a lush, light turquoise. The bathrooms sparkled with white tile floors and turquoise backsplashes. An enormous, jetted tub took center stage in the master bath, and French doors opened to a patio off the master bedroom, which overlooked the tropical, backyard setting.

"Let's go back downstairs, and I will try to envision the living room with off-white paint and light turquoise carpet." Millicent led the way. Standing in the middle of the room, she stared at the large, rounded window, then at the brick fireplace.

"What's through there?" She pointed to an archway next to the stairs.

Christine swallowed hard. "That's a bonus room that the owner used as a studio."

Marge headed for the arch and peeked inside, Millicent close behind her. "There's plenty of light." Marge pursed her lips. The giant skylight and windows let in ample daylight, and the walls were mostly white, but the white tile floor had been destroyed. "It has potential. Can we walk around the backyard?"

Retracing their steps through the kitchen and exiting through the French doors, they stood on the back patio, overlooking the pool and a verdant landscape of tropical plants.

"How long have these plants been here?" Millicent asked. "Have they made it through the winter?"

Christine looked uncomfortable. "I believe he had the yard re-landscaped last spring. You might need to cover some of the plants in plastic when it freezes."

"I love this house, except for the downstairs walls and carpet. If the owner will either have them repaired or deduct the cost from the price of the house, I am prepared to purchase it. If he opts to make repairs, the walls will have to be stripped and repainted so the dark colors do not show through. Also, I will need some information and instructions regarding the plants. I would be very disappointed if they all died during the winter."

Christine grimaced. "The walls in the living room, bonus room, and stairwell and the carpet in the living room and stairwell should match the upstairs and the floor in the bonus room retiled?"

"Yes. And if you like, I can have my contractor come and give you an estimate."

"That might be a good idea."

"Also, please let me know if any other homes in this area are for sale."

"Yes, ma'am. I'll be looking forward to hearing from your contractor.

Marge and Millicent walked back up the street to Marge's house.

"What's your honest opinion?"

"The house, excluding the artistic atrocity, is stunning. It's priced over market value, so he was doubtless cognizant of the requisite renovations."

Staring, Millicent said, "Could you repeat that?"

"We should take our repose, so we are ready to go at six," Marge said. Rarely could she remember the exact phrase she used, and she didn't have the energy to try. She entered her room and laid on her bed, forgetting to set her alarm as was her wont.

At a quarter to six, Millicent knocked on Marge's bedroom door, to no avail. She could hear Marge's rhythmic snores from within, so she knocked louder. "Marge. Time to wake up," she called. "Marge?" Carefully opening the door and peeking inside, she found Marge flailing in her blankets. "Marge?" she whispered. "Are you okay?"

Gradually Marge surfaced from sleep and stared at Millicent. "Sorry. I was ensnared in the roots of a malicious tree. Is Joey here?"

"You have about ten minutes to get ready before he arrives."

"Thank you."

Shaking her head, Millicent closed the door and went downstairs to brew a pot of coffee. Marge could be completely incomprehensible at times. Ensnared in tree roots? Was she dreaming? She finished preparing the coffee and went to answer the door. "Good timing. You look refreshed."

"Yes, I'm feeling much better. How about you? Did you find time to rest?"

"I did. Marge is getting ready. Would you like a cup of coffee?"

"Sounds great. Did you like the house?"

"I loved it, but it has some flaws. We'll have to negotiate."

"I imagine the owner anticipated that. The house is priced high."

Millicent nodded. *That's what she meant. Why couldn't she just say that?* Then her eyes widened as Marge skipped down the stairs in the brightest lime-green pantsuit she had ever seen. "What *are* you wearing, Marge?"

"Isn't it beautiful? It's my favorite." Marge grinned.

"Perfectly festive," Joey said, grinning back.

Millicent held her tongue. Marge had some fine qualities, even if fashion was not one of them.

They arrived at the church early. The doors to the vestibule were unlocked, which Marge considered a good sign. The sanctuary glowed as the late afternoon sun shone through a stained-glass window behind the chancel, and the wood floor gleamed in the light.

Millicent went to make sure their room was set up properly, and Joey said, "I need to prepare for this evening, Marge, so why don't you play the piano for a while?"

She grinned. "I haven't played for ages. That sounds invigorating." Joey left the sanctuary as Marge headed for the baby grand piano and gently opened the top. She sat on the bench, reaching for a hymnal and flipping through to *How Great Thou Art*, one of her favorites. Singing loudly and a little off-key, she played a dramatic rendition and felt her spirits rise exponentially. Continuing with *What a Friend We Have in Jesus*, then *Standing on the Promises*, she was startled when Joey called to her that the first members were pulling into the parking lot.

By six-thirty, the entire Bible study group, even those whose attendance was sporadic, was seated around the large table in the meeting room. Marge had pulled Harriet aside and explained what happened so she wouldn't be shocked in front of the other members. Joey stood and thanked everyone for coming. He explained the situation and asked them to show their love and support for Pastor Greg.

"What about the church funds?" asked Mr. Flannigan.

"We will address that later," Marge said. "Harriet is a master at organizing fundraisers, and we can also report the con artist, but right now, it is our Christian duty to show Pastor Greg God's love and compassion, just as God showed us when he sent Jesus to die for our sins."

"Anyone who does not agree with our plan of action should excuse him or herself this evening. We must show a united front. Is everyone agreed?" He asked for a show of hands, and it was unanimous.

"I'll go get him," Joey said. He left the meeting and went next door. Greg was tossing and turning in his sleep with a tormented look on his face. Hating to wake him, Joey said his name gently, then laid a hand on his arm. The pastor sat up with a start. "It's time for Bible study," Joey said.

Groaning, Greg got out of bed and went into the bathroom to splash some water on his face and brush his teeth. "I feel like I'm about to face a firing squad."

"You aren't. We have apprised everyone of the situation, and they have all vowed to lend their support. All you need to do is show up."

They walked back to the church and entered the meeting room, where every last member stood and offered their pastor a handshake or a hug. His face crumpled, and tears rolled down his face as his flock showered him with God's love and forgiveness. Swiping at his tears, he said, "I don't deserve you."

"Isn't that the point of Christianity?" Millicent asked. "None of us deserve God's love and forgiveness, yet he gifts us with them every day. Come sit with me and hold my hand."

Everyone took their seats, and Joey opened his Bible.

"This evening we are going to talk about God's plan for us. Let's begin with Jeremiah 29:11, "For I know the plans I have for you," declares the Lord, "plans to prosper you and not to harm you, plans to give you hope and a future." And Romans 8:28, "And we know that for those who love God, all things work together for good, for those who are called according to his purpose." Joey looked up at the assembled group. "What happens when we think we are following God's path, but things don't turn out how we think they should? Does that mean we misinterpreted his will, or is it possible that we don't understand the bigger picture? Perhaps God, in his omniscience, used this painful setback to teach us all something or to bring us closer together. We may find our faith stronger and our understanding of God's love and forgiveness greater." He paused. "I invite you to share your thoughts or relevant scripture on this topic."

A lively discussion ensued, lasting so long that Marge called to order pizza. Members shared not only their philosophical thoughts on the matter but also recounted stories that illustrated bad decisions and good, with unexpected results. The group was drawn closer together, and Joey was pleased to see that Greg's healing had begun. He looked around at the smiling faces and gave thanks in his heart.

Chapter 28

The next morning, Marge and Joey chose to forego yoga and attend the ten o'clock Aikido class instead. After breakfasting with Millicent, Joey went home to change, and they met outside at nine-thirty. The walk passed quickly, Marge excitedly discoursing a mile a minute. Joey, amused, held his tongue and hoped the class was a positive experience for both of them. When they arrived, the school was once again closed. "Do you suppose it opens at ten?" Marge asked, peering through the window into the darkened lobby.

"If we had already paid, I would think it was a scam. But since that is not the case, I believe it may be poor management or an undisciplined sensei, which is not a good sign either."

Marge sat on the stoop, frowned, and dialed the number on the window sign. When it went to voicemail, she said, "Hello. We are at the school for the ten o'clock adult beginner Aikido lesson, and no one is here. I was wondering if the schedule has changed. Thank you." She disconnected to find Joey staring at her. "What?"

"You didn't say who was calling, Marge."

She shrugged. "At least they know someone came to class. Is it too early for lunch?"

"A little. We could go home and do our yoga."

"Or we could go sit in the park."

"For an hour?"

"Or until we get hungry enough to forget about the time." She grinned, and Joey couldn't help but laugh. She got up, dusting off her bottom, and offered Joey a hand. Pulling just a little too forcefully, she managed to fall over backward, but luckily, Joey grabbed his walker and was able to right himself.

175

"We need to work on that," Marge said, sitting on the sidewalk and laughing. "One of us is going to break something. Today, I will demonstrate the downward dog," she declared. She rolled onto her hands and knees, then straightened her legs.

"Bravo." Joey clapped enthusiastically until he saw someone glare at him suspiciously. Marge, oblivious to disapproval, stood with a bow. He clapped again, although more quietly.

"To the park!" Marge strode down the street. Joey ambled after her, knowing that she would stop and wait at the corner. As he approached, Marge was engaged in an animated conversation. Joey stopped and wrinkled his brow, staring as she appeared to be conversing with a ghost. Turning her head mid-sentence, she stopped with her mouth open. She looked around her, then back at Joey as he approached. "Was I talking to myself that whole time?"

"I'm afraid so." Joey smiled.

"Now I have to try to remember what I was talking about."

"I'm sure you will."

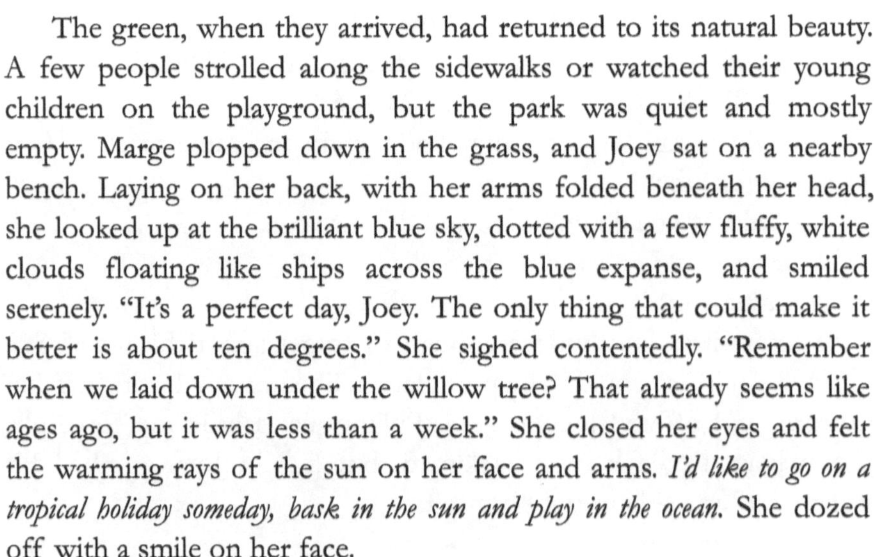

The green, when they arrived, had returned to its natural beauty. A few people strolled along the sidewalks or watched their young children on the playground, but the park was quiet and mostly empty. Marge plopped down in the grass, and Joey sat on a nearby bench. Laying on her back, with her arms folded beneath her head, she looked up at the brilliant blue sky, dotted with a few fluffy, white clouds floating like ships across the blue expanse, and smiled serenely. "It's a perfect day, Joey. The only thing that could make it better is about ten degrees." She sighed contentedly. "Remember when we laid down under the willow tree? That already seems like ages ago, but it was less than a week." She closed her eyes and felt the warming rays of the sun on her face and arms. *I'd like to go on a tropical holiday someday, bask in the sun and play in the ocean.* She dozed off with a smile on her face.

"Marge?" she heard her name being called from far away. The man in the rowboat, out in the ocean, was waving his hands. How did he know her name? He moved his mouth, but she heard no sound. "Marge." Now his lips weren't moving, but he was sounding impatient. "Marge, wake up." She opened her eyes and regained her sense of time and space, then turned her head to look at Joey. "Was I snoring?"

"Almost imperceptibly, but I'm getting hungry." He patted his stomach, and Marge sat up.

"What time is it?"

"It's almost noon. The bewitching hour."

"Let's go get some sustenance. We have been doing quite a bit of walking; it builds up the appetite."

Entering the Fireside Café felt familiar and welcoming to Marge, the tinkling bell on the door, Sally's friendly greeting, and the cheerful fire were comforting. She greeted familiar faces as she headed for her favorite table, noting that the café was once again peaceful and sparsely populated since the festival had concluded. Sally also appeared much more relaxed and approached their table with menus. "You probably don't need these." She smiled. "The special today is sesame chicken, fried rice, and asparagus."

"Perfect," Joey said.

Pausing, Marge said, "I don't know…" She thought a moment. "Yes, okay. I'll have that too. Otherwise, it's too hard to decide."

Sally smiled and nodded before returning to the kitchen and reappearing almost immediately with two small lacquer bowls. "I forgot to mention that your meal comes with a bowl of hot and sour soup. Chuck likes food themes, and today is Chinese.

Marge thanked her and tried the soup, nodding her approval. Sally left again, and Marge said, "En route, I was pondering our predilection for the Fireside and deliberating whether we should diversify, but I have determined that it's unnecessary. The Fireside is comfortable and has a broad assortment of culinary selections."

"I agree. Italian one day, Chinese the next. And if for some reason, we don't want the special, there is an entire menu, largely unexplored."

Returning with their entrees, Sally placed their plates on the table and said, "Enjoy!"

Marge took a bite of her chicken. "Mmmm." Her eyes rolled back. "I can't believe I almost declined this delicacy."

Too busy eating to reply, Joey remained silent.

Scooping some fried rice with her spoon, Marge shook her head and stared at Joey. "Did you hear that?"

"Hear what?" he mumbled around his soup bowl.

"I must remind myself to take local gossip with a grain of salt. Are you about ready to go?"

"Almost. Should we take something home for Millicent?"

"She is marvelously self-sufficient in the kitchen and has likely eaten."

"Let's head home then and rest up for this evening."

* * *

The walk home was pleasant, but Joey could feel the change in the air. The days were becoming shorter and chillier, and soon they would be wearing hats and gloves, wishing for summer to return. Except Marge, perhaps. Marge loved snow and howling storms. She enjoyed sitting in front of the fireplace with a cup of cocoa after building a gravity-defying snowman. *I like the fire and cocoa part.*

"Look, Joey." Marge waved her arm high above her head.

"Is that Millicent?"

"Yes. And she's walking with Mrs. Waddle and Sir Chewalot." She waved again. "Hello, Millicent, Mrs. Waddle. How are you enjoying this lovely day?"

Mrs. Waddle, ever loquacious, began a long explanation about how she saw Millicent out walking and asked to join her.

Millicent smiled weakly at Marge. "And then, as I was inspecting the roses for signs of frostbite, there she was, looking up at the house next door, and I thought…"

Marge glanced at Millicent and at the house in question.

"…she's probably lonely since Marge and Joey are out. I bet she'd like a bit of company. And when I asked her, she agreed that she would. So I-"

"Bessy, dear, I hate to interrupt, but I'm feeling a little tired. Would it be alright if we finished our walk another time?"

"Oh, yes. I'm sorry, Mrs. Beaumonde. I had a lovely time. I do hope we become neighbors."

"I'm sure that would be delightful," Millicent said kindly. "Thank you for keeping me company this afternoon."

"It's good to see you, Mrs. Waddle," Marge said before resuming their walk home.

Joey had stood silently throughout the exchange, having learned the difficulty of extricating himself after engaging Bessy Waddle in any type of conversation. Marge and Millicent, it appeared, were much more adept at the art of disentanglement.

<hr>

Greeted at the door by a demanding feline, Marge went directly to the pantry and grabbed the cat food. Fluster headbutted her shin and meowed loudly. "He's on a schedule," she told Millicent, and I'm late. Speaking of which, have you eaten lunch?"

"Yes, I ate early. I was hungry for some reason. Perhaps it's all the excitement. My daily life is a lot quieter when I'm left to my own devices. You and Joey keep very busy, don't you."

"Yes, I suppose we do, especially during holidays and festivals. Should we take a breather before the party this evening?" Looking around, she said, "Where is Joey?"

"I'm here." He entered the kitchen and sat at the table.

"I think I could use a lie down too. Why don't we reconvene at six? Don't forget to set your alarm, Marge."

"I'm not feeling fatigued. A cat nap will do."

Millicent smiled. "I'll make sure she's up."

Determined to prove them wrong, Marge took off her shoes and lay down on top of her covers to rest. *I won't even sleep. It will be me waking Millicent after her outing with Mrs. Waddle.* And then her eyes closed, and she was out.

Millicent roused Marge from a deep sleep, amazed at how she could slumber so soundly at any time of day. When Marge finally appeared in the kitchen, Millicent and Joey were having coffee and discussing their plans for the evening.

"It will take us about half an hour to walk to your house, so we will arrive in plenty of time."

"Walk? Isn't it awfully far?"

"You walked here the other day," he replied.

"Yes, but I stopped at the Fireside. Couldn't we drive there?"

"We could, but then we wouldn't be able to enjoy the cocktails."

"I'll change shoes then." Millicent went back upstairs to retrieve her walking shoes and returned after a moment. "Ready."

The three of them headed toward the town square, and as they approached the Fireside café, Peter pulled up beside them and asked them if they would like a ride.

"Yes, please," Millicent raised a hand.

Marge glanced at Joey, who shrugged. They climbed into the back seat, greeted Sally, and sat back for a ride up the hill.

"You look beautiful, Sally," Marge said. "That is a lovely shade of green."

"Thank you. I was expecting to be wined and dined."

"You will be cocktail-ed and hors d'oeuvre-d." Joey winked, and Sally giggled.

Parking at the edge of the Beaumondes' circular drive, Peter helped his passengers disembark and took Sally's hand. It was their first date, after all.

Chapter 29

A butler, hired for the occasion, greeted them at the door and led them into the elegant, formal parlor, complete with fireplace, piano, and bar. The bartender stood at the ready, and Daisy circulated with trays of small finger foods. Millicent was pleased and amused by her guests' reactions to her efforts.

When everyone had arrived and received a drink and a small plate of food, Millicent strode to the fireplace and spoke loudly enough to draw the attention of her guests. "Welcome, everyone. The purpose of our little party is two-fold; it's a welcome home party for Elizabeth (polite smattering of applause) and a discussion about recent events. But before we begin, I have an announcement to make. It's not for public consumption, but I feel better sharing it amongst friends." She paused and drew a breath. "Recently, I have not felt safe in my home. Family members have died or been injured, and I have been privy to conversations about the possibility of declaring me incompetent and drawing up a Power of Attorney. I have been treated like a child and feel like I'm a means to an end, so I paid a visit to my attorney and asked him how to protect myself.

"The result is a new will and a family trust. Everything I own has been placed in a trust to be held for my remaining family members and distributed on my oldest grandchild's fortieth birthday. If my death is ruled suspicious, everything will go to my good friend Marge Bumfuzzle who will, I'm sure, put it to good use. I will be selling this house and moving to a smaller one. The milk plant will remain open, and my daughter, Elizabeth, may accept this house or the factory in lieu of a future inheritance if she so chooses."

Elizabeth fainted, which caused a flurry of activity. Peter rushed over to check her breathing and pulse, and Chief Lloyd took her a glass of water, handing it to her after she came to.

She looked around for Millicent and said, "Mother, I'm so sorry we made you feel like you had to protect yourself. Reginald was always trying to figure out how to get his hands on more cash, but I would never have allowed him to do such a thing."

"I'm glad to hear that, Elizabeth. We will have further conversations in private, but I wanted to make everyone aware of my new arrangements so that there will be no more plotting or tragedies. Now, without further ado, I will hand the floor over to Ms. Bumfuzzle." Millicent smiled at Marge and raised her glass.

Marge was a little nervous, which resulted in several stinkers, but she put on her proverbial teacher's hat and addressed her audience. "The Beaumondes have suffered the demise of two family members in one week. The first to pass was Gavin, the long-lost first child of Millicent Beaumonde, and I construe that his fate was accidental."

Responses from those in attendance varied greatly. Chief Lloyd, standing near the bar, scowled into his glass. Sally, sitting on a loveseat next to Peter, leaned toward him with her lips pursed and said something in his ear. He shook his head. Oliver and James, sitting in recliners, were unfamiliar with the case and merely displayed natural curiosity.

After a pause, Marge continued. "Elizabeth arrived at Gavin's bedroom door with a bottle of wine and two glasses to inquire about his intentions. The conversation turned unpleasant, and Elizabeth left with her glass of wine when he began to taunt her. Unbeknownst to the family, he was taking a medication which has negative effects when combined with wine. Heavy consumption would have brought on fatally high blood pressure, but it's possible that no one in the family was aware of his passing when they left the house in the morning."

Everyone present looked at each other with surprise and murmured amongst themselves.

Chief Lloyd said, "An interesting theory, but unlikely. Did he hide in the closet when his chest pains began?"

Marge smiled serenely. "When Gavin's girlfriend slipped into his room that morning, she found him lifeless. Recognizing the scent of Elizabeth's distinctive perfume in his bedroom, her grief rapidly transformed into fury. Transferring his body to the closet and spraying Elizabeth's perfume inside, she then broke a downstairs window and telephoned the police to report a break-in."

"Who was his girlfriend?" Elizabeth asked. "She must have been at least my age since Gavin was older." She paused. "And how did she recognize my perfume?"

"You disclosed the theft of a newly purchased bottle shortly after Gavin arrived. I believe he appropriated your perfume for his girlfriend."

Elizabeth scowled. "I knew he was no good."

Chief Lloyd tapped his foot and looked at his watch. Glancing around the room, Marge once again took up her tale. "Gavin's girlfriend is clever, and she was enraged for two reasons, one being the perceived murder of her lover and the other, the result of Reginald's infidelities. She determined that eliminating her enemies, one by murder and the other by incarceration, would be an appropriate punishment for their crimes.

"It's getting late," Sally complained. "Are we almost done here?"

"Not quite. Our murderess' first step was to make Reginald's favorite cookies, which were unusual and made for him by Elizabeth on a recurring basis. She accrued some of Gavin's medication and borrowed a block of cheese from Elizabeth. The remainder was effortless. Her best friend apprised her of Reginald's late-night meeting, and her father's badge granted her access to the milk plant." Sally's face had been gradually gaining color, and she finally reacted. "I don't know where you got your information, but you are obviously describing me. You have no proof of any of this. I could sue you for slander."

Marge studied Sally's face. "After Gavin arrived, you visited the Beaumonde house bearing a cake. You told Mrs. Beaumonde senior that you and Gavin were friends, but you neglected to mention the nature of your relationship."

"We were just friends."

"Then perhaps you could elucidate the photo inside this locket" Marge held up Fluster's treasure.

"Give me that! Where did you get it?" Sally rose and lurched toward Marge, but Peter pulled her back.

"The inscription on the back reads 'Love, Gavin,' and the picture shows the two of you sharing a kiss. Fluster unearthed the locket and concealed it under my sofa. I will leave it with Chief Lloyd as evidence." Marge nodded at the chief, who was looking like thunder.

"To resume, you purloined your father's badge and conveyed the toxic cookies to Reginald's office. He had chronic high blood pressure, and by introducing the medication into the cheesy cookies, you ensured it would rise fatally. You lingered, with the intention of retrieving the plate of cookies once he was dead or dying, but you heard footsteps in the plant, so you spritzed the perfume, seized the trophy, and extinguished the light. Incidentally, you discovered Elizabeth's bracelet and retained it for future use."

Tears were coursing down Elizabeth's cheeks, and Oliver was staring at his daughter in horror.

"What? Dad! You don't believe her?"

Marge proceeded inexorably. "James was not your intended suspect, so you assaulted him from behind and spritzed more perfume. You concealed yourself when you became aware of our presence. Did you deliberately open the door to the vat to lure us in?"

"I have no idea what you're talking about."

Peter sat very still, nervously glancing at Sally from the corner of his eye.

"You locked us in the vat and dropped the bracelet on the floor to provide further 'evidence.' By then, it was getting late, and you had to get home before your father became cognizant of his missing badge. On the way, you secreted the trophy and Joey's walker in the boot of Elizabeth's car. What you didn't grasp, however, was that Reginald had driven Elizabeth's car to the plant."

"Only you could take evidence that points at a killer and twist it around toward someone else."

Oliver sat pale and shaking. "Why?" he whispered hoarsely.

"Dad, how can you even listen to this?" Sally cried.

"My badge was in a slightly different place that morning, and I thought it was strange that the car was warm. And you were baking the day before, but whatever you baked was gone. You didn't clean up your mess."

"Didn't you care that he took mom away from us?"

"I didn't know it was him until recently, but yes, I cared. I wouldn't have killed him over it, though. It was her choice to leave."

"It wasn't Gavin's choice to die."

"Ms. Bumfuzzle said it was an accident. Didn't he know he shouldn't drink wine with his medication?"

"He was a recovering alcoholic. He couldn't help himself. She pressured him into having that first drink."

"I didn't know," Elizabeth said quietly.

Millicent stood next to her and took her hand.

"Well, it solved a problem for you, didn't it." Sally's face was red with anger, and tears rolled down her cheeks. "Your family took everything from me."

"You decided to play God and punish them by killing Reginald and framing Elizabeth for his murder. It was a clever plan, but you overdid the evidence. No one, even the most idiotic criminal, would be that obvious. He or she would possess some measure of self-preservation," Marge said.

Sally stood angrily and stomped toward the door,

but Chief Lloyd stopped her. "Sally Drake, I'm arresting you for the murder of Reginald Beaumonde."

"No!" she screamed and tried to pull away.

Cuffing her, the chief said, "Read her the Miranda, Locke."

As Peter approached and began the recitation, Sally glared at him and attempted to speak over him. "I thought you cared about me, but you're nothing but a weak, stupid auntie's boy." She continued yelling as Peter, and the chief led her from the room.

Chapter 30

As if someone flipped a switch, when Sally was led from the room, everyone began speaking at once. Marge ignored them all and walked over to sit beside Oliver, who sat bereft, his face drained of color. "I'm sorry," she said.

Looking at the floor, shoulders hunched, he said, "How could I have been so blind? She seemed so strong. I let her take on all her mother's responsibilities and didn't give her a thought. I failed her."

Marge laid her hand on his. "Perhaps they will get her some help. That level of planning and vengeance is not an ordinary response to loss."

He stood. "I'll excuse myself; I think I need to be home with Seth right now."

"Of course. Please let me or Joey know if you need anything."

She watched him leave and turned her attention to the others.

"Are you okay?" Joey sat next to her and handed her a glass of whiskey.

Millicent gazed at her in awe. "That's why you wanted Chief Lloyd here. She was Peter's date."

"Thank you for clearing my name," Elizabeth said shakily. "Poor Reginald must have died thinking I poisoned him."

"Freida will never believe it." James shook his head. "Tell us how you figured it out."

Marge silently took a sip of her whiskey, then another. "So sad." She took another sip.

"Well?" James said expectantly.

She sighed. "When I examined all the evidence, she was the only person who could have done it, and she might have gotten away with it if she hadn't been so obviously pointing at Elizabeth. As Millicent asserted, it was too much. No one could be that careless.

The perfume, the bracelet, the cookies, hiding the weapon in her car. And who else knew Gavin, knew Reginald would be at the plant and had access, borrowed the block of cheese, and liked to bake? When I found the locket yesterday, I was sure."

"We didn't see the locket," Millicent said.

Marge handed it to her.

Brushing a stray tear, Millicent said, "Giving him up for adoption was the most difficult thing I've ever done. I would have enjoyed getting to know him, hearing about his life, including him in family events."

"I'm so sorry, mother. I just didn't know."

"I know, dear. I'm not blaming you."

"Are you really moving?"

"Yes. I've been staying with Marge, and I really love her little house."

"And I can keep this one? It's the only home the kids, and I have ever known. You will come to visit and have family dinners here, won't you?"

"Yes, but you understand that it costs money to live in this big house. You will have to find some form of income."

"Will you explain that to me later? I've never paid much attention."

"Yes, I know. I'll help you figure it out." Millicent patted her hand. "Where did those hors d'oeuvres go? I'm feeling a little peckish."

The party continued, but Marge asked Joey if they could go home, so he made their excuses, and they slipped away. They were mostly silent on the way home, and Joey accompanied Marge to her door. "Will you be alright?" he asked.

Marge nodded. "Thank you, Joey. Yoga tomorrow?"

"See you at nine."

She went inside and locked her door before heading for the kitchen to feed Fluster.

Sitting at the kitchen table, she pondered Sally's rage and the havoc she wreaked. *In trying to destroy the Beaumonde family, she inadvertently destroyed her own as well. Poor Peter. The Sally he thought he loved didn't exist.* Marge rose and ascended the stairs with a heavy heart.

The next morning, Marge woke with a spring in her step. The night before seemed like a distant nightmare. Reality was morning yoga with Joey, and she was ready to try disc two. She brought up her Facetime app, and there was his lopsided grin. "Are you sure?" was his response to her suggestion.

"We can at least try it. We've been doing disc one for a long time."

"I'm game if you are."

Marge thought it was probably lucky that Millicent wasn't there because the groans and grunts were particularly emphatic that morning, but they made it all the way through the workout. "I might not be able to move tomorrow."

"You will… probably." Joey laughed. See you at breakfast."

They disconnected, and Marge showered and started a pot of coffee. *Today is a bacon and egg day.*

Joey knocked and let himself in, only to find her standing at the kitchen counter, staring at a broken egg at her feet. "Marge?"

She looked up at him with tears in her eyes. He put his walker aside and, avoiding the egg, hugged her. He hugged her until she was all cried out, then helped her sit at the table, where she sat watching him cook breakfast for the very first time.

He gently set a plate of food and a cup of coffee in front of her then got his own, fed Fluster, who was body slamming his shins with impatience and sat down across the table.

"I didn't know you could cook." She sniffled.

"I can't really, but I've watched you enough times that I can at least make eggs and bacon. What happened?"

"I don't know. I woke up feeling happy that everything was back to normal. I love our morning routine. The sun was shining, everything was splendid, then I dropped an egg, and it broke, just like those families broke, and then I broke too."

Joey nodded gravely. "I think you denied your feelings last night, and they caught up with you. That was traumatic, especially since we are all friends."

"It didn't seem real when I was trying to figure it out. It was a puzzle I was trying to solve. But the reality was painful; seeing Oliver's self-blame and broken heart was too much."

Someone knocked on the front door, and Joey said, "Do you want me to ignore that?"

"No, it might be someone who needs us."

Joey went to answer the door and returned with Peter. He looked unhappy, with shoulders drooping and bloodshot eyes, but was concerned when he saw Marge had been crying. He stooped next to her chair and asked, "Are you okay, Aunt Marge?"

"I'll be fine. How about you?"

"It might take some time, but I'll be fine, too. They've sent Sally to the psychiatric hospital for evaluation. She seems to have had a complete mental breakdown."

"I thought that might be the case. I hope she will recover."

"Me too, but I realized that I never really knew her. She was in love with Gavin and just using me for information. I feel like a fool."

"If that's all you feel, then you are lucky."

Peter hung his head and mumbled, "Not all."

"I know, dear." She smoothed his hair. "Solving crime in a small town, where friends and neighbors are involved, is not for the faint-hearted."

"It would be easier in a big city."

"Possibly. But who better than you to make sure our loved ones stay safe?"

Peter smiled weakly. "Do you have any leftovers?"

"Luckily, today's master chef cooked for three. Grab yourself a plate."

The speed and voracity with which Peter ate were akin to a competition. Joey, a fan of Molly Schuyler and Joel Hansen, watched with fascination. The quantity, of course, was not nearly the same, but the enthusiasm was there.

He was about to ask if Peter had ever considered entering a food challenge, but Peter laid down his fork and said, "Thank you for breakfast. I must get back to work."

Joey watched him leave and gaped at Marge. "That was impressive. We should have an eating contest during the next festival; hot dogs or hot peppers."

Marge's eyes sparkled. "Let's mention it to Mayor Wright. What's on the agenda today?"

"For the first time in over a week, I am happy to report that our agenda is clear. Perhaps we could build a fire and read for a while, then walk over to the Fireside for lunch."

"That sounds lovely. I have a stack of books waiting to be read."

Chapter 31

Millicent sat down for breakfast with Elizabeth, prepared to show her a summary of their monthly bills, but before she did, Elizabeth said, "I don't want you to move. It won't be the same without you. I know we haven't been very nice to you, but you don't want to live all alone, do you?"

"I've always hated this big house and the loneliness I've experienced here. I would much rather have a cozy home closer to my friends."

"Can't you invite them here? And we can do more family things. I know I've been caught up in what Reginald was doing and our social status, but I was wrong. Our focus should be on our family and raising the children right. I can't help but wonder how terrible I would feel if I was in Oliver's place. I need to make some changes, and I don't think I can do it alone. You can still explain our expenses, and I can get a job. I think the kids should find jobs too, but I wish you would stay and be part of the family unit."

"I'm surprised. That's not the reaction I expected from you."

"I know. I'm so sorry for how I've behaved. I don't have any excuse."

"I'll need to think about it. I found a house that I really like."

"That's fair. I understand, but I don't want you to go. I'll miss you."

They ate in silence for a few minutes, then Millicent handed Elizabeth the list of expenses. "These are average monthly costs for running the house. You'll want to understand them whether or not I stay. I've listed mandatory costs, such as utilities, taxes, and insurance, and optional costs, like staff, with totals for each."

Elizabeth took the sheet of paper and examined it with wide eyes.

"This is more than a lot of the monthly salaries at the milk plant."

"The money that pays for these expenses and the allowance I have been giving you comes from the interest on our savings. Any profit that comes from the milk plant goes toward necessary upgrades and repairs. Reginald was stealing from the plant, which meant it was no longer sustainable, and you have been complaining about your monthly allowance. If I start taking out principal, the interest will no longer be able to support us, and I will have to use more and more principal for monthly expenses. Eventually, we will be broke and unable to keep the house. Do you understand?"

"Yes. The reason we can live the way we do is because you have been careful with the finances. And our selfishness must have been very frustrating." She hung her head. "I didn't understand, and I didn't care. I'm sorry, mother."

"I won't insist you get a job, but your allowance is twice as much as most people earn each month, and it should be more than enough. I don't know what you spend it on, but you have been extravagant and wasteful."

Nodding, Elizabeth said, "Why do you like Marge so much? She's weird."

"She has a good heart." Millicent thought a moment. "I went to her because I trusted her, but I learned a lot about her during my stay. She may be eccentric, but she is also smart and fun. I think you would like her too if you could look past her outer shell."

Elizabeth thought about that for a moment. "Will you show me the house you want to buy?"

Millicent paused. "It has some cosmetic problems downstairs. I'm negotiating repairs, but if you would like to see it, I'll ask the agent for another showing."

"I would like that, not to try to change your mind, just because I'd like to see what you find attractive. I wonder what kind of living space you would prefer to this house where I've lived my entire life."

After finishing their breakfast, Elizabeth watched, entranced, as Millicent cleared the table and put the dishes in the dishwasher. Millicent then called Christine and made an appointment to see the house again. "We can go over now if you like. The agent will meet us there."

After a relaxing morning reading silently together, Marge and Joey left for the Fireside Café. "The Fireside won't be the same without Sally," Marge said sadly. As she pulled the door open for Joey, the little bell on the door gave its usual jingle. The restaurant looked and sounded exactly the same, and when Marge looked into the restaurant, she saw a cheerful young lady with a welcoming smile on her face, saying, "Good afternoon. Where would you like to be seated?"

"In the middle, please," Marge said with a bemused look on her face.

"I'm Helen," the young lady told them on the way. She handed them menus after they were seated. "I'm Curtis' niece, and I'm new, so it will take some time for me to remember everyone's names."

"Marge Bumfuzzle and Joey Cattywampus," Joey supplied.

Helen laughed. "That's great." Then she blushed when she saw he was serious. "Nice to meet you. Do you know what you'd like to order? I hear the menu hasn't changed in decades."

"What is the special?" Joey asked.

"No special today. The chef is out with a cold."

He looked at Marge in horror. "Now, what will we do?"

"We always order the special. We'll need to study the menu."

"Take your time. I'll check back in a few minutes." Helen walked back to the front counter.

"That family has strong genes. Helen must be Sally's cousin." Marge opened her menu, and the bell on the door jangled.

Not hearing the familiar greeting, she looked up to see Helen and Peter frozen in their tracks, gazing at each other. "Oh my." She returned to her menu. "Take your time. She might be a while."

Joey chuckled, then looked at his menu and frowned. "How can we possibly decide? It will take half an hour just to read the menu."

"Let's look at the headings first and narrow it down. For example, would you like pasta? A sandwich? Chinese?"

"If Chuck isn't here, a sandwich is probably safest."

Marge nodded and glanced over at the front counter where Peter was in deep conversation with Helen, then back at the menu. "Let's get two sandwiches and split them so we can try both. You pick one, and I'll pick one."

"How about a club sandwich?"

"Yes, and a… no… wait a moment… a tuna melt. I had better inform the cook because Helen is preoccupied." Marge walked back to the kitchen window and gave the substitute chef their order. As she returned to the table, Helen blushed and raced after her. "I'm so sorry. Can I get you something to drink? Coffee?"

"Yes, coffee would be lovely, and water, please."

"The same for you, sir?"

"Yes, please. And won't you ask Sergeant Locke to join us?"

<hr>

Watching Helen return from Marge and Joey's table, Peter wasn't surprised when she told him they had invited him to lunch. He asked her on a date, ordered a sandwich, and strode over to the table. "Hello, Aunt Marge, Joey." Taking a seat, he blushed when they both grinned at him, then leaned in. "She's just like Sally, only she doesn't make me nervous."

"Hopefully, not *just* like Sally."

"That's probably why Sally made you nervous. She was hiding an enormous secret." Joey added.

Peter smiled contentedly. "Helen is very nice."

"Do you have any news about Sally?" Marge asked.

"Yes, she's been admitted to the psychiatric hospital as a .370 patient."

"What does that mean?"

"She has been deemed unfit to stand trial, so she'll receive medication and therapy, along with legal skills classes, until she is deemed able."

Marge nodded. "I was hoping she would receive psychiatric care."

Helen arrived at their table with two coffees and a soda. "I'll be right back with the sandwiches. I couldn't carry everything at once."

Peter popped out of his chair. "Let me help you." Following her to the counter, he took a plate, his fingers brushing against hers. *Now I know what butterflies mean.* Setting his plate on the table, he remained standing until Helen left, staring after her as if in a trance.

"He's got it bad," Joey whispered in Marge's ear.

"Amazing resilience." Marge swapped half of her sandwich with his. "I hope Pastor Greg is also recovering." Looking up when the bell tinkled, she saw Harriet scan the restaurant and head for their table.

"May I join you?"

"Certainly. What are your plans for today?"

"I tried to bake an apple pie for Greg, but it was terrible. I thought I might buy one here instead. Would you go with me to visit? I don't want to frighten him."

"That's a lovely idea, Harriet. He will probably benefit from seeing friends."

"We could take him lunch as well." Joey took a bite of the second sandwich. "Which one do you like best, Marge?"

"The club. Have you eaten, Harriet?"

"No, but I don't want to hold you up."

"Go ahead and order, and we'll order a club sandwich to go." Joey waved at Helen. "Do you know what you want? There's no special today."

Her brow furrowed. "No special? That does complicate things. I guess I'll have a club sandwich, too since both of you are enjoying it."

Helen appeared at the table and introduced herself to Harriet.

"Nice to meet you. I'm Harriet, and I'll have a club sandwich."

"We'll take a second club sandwich and an apple pie to go," Joey added.

"And could you refill my coffee, please?" Marge asked.

"I'll be right back with that. Will you have coffee, too, Harriet?"

"No, thank you. Just water."

Helen smiled at Peter and left to get coffee.

After lunch, the three said goodbye to Peter and got into Harriet's white Prius for the short drive to the rectory. Marge was pleased to see the curtains open. The doors to the sanctuary were also open, and the message on the sign had been changed. It read, *Above all, keep loving one another earnestly, since love covers a multitude of sins. I Peter 4:8* "Look, Joey." Marge pointed.

He read the sign and smiled. "I think he will be okay."

Harriet had entered the sanctuary and stuck her head through the open doors. "Where's that food?"

"Coming," Marge sang. "We were just admiring the sign."

Chapter 32

Pastor Greg was quite obviously in the middle of a cleaning project but had set aside his accoutrements upon their arrival. "Hello, friends. I'm glad to see you today."

"Does that mean you need help?" Joey chuckled.

Greg laughed too. "No, I'm just happy to see you."

"We brought you some lunch since we were at the Fireside, and Harriet brought you one of their apple pies."

"Thank you. I am getting a little hungry. I suppose you saw the kitchen. I must do some shopping." He accepted the sandwich from Joey. "Come on back to my office. I'm afraid it's a horrible disaster." He found chairs for everyone and sat at his desk. "I had no idea how much Harriet had taken on. I am lost without you, Harriet. Could I offer you a paid position as church secretary once we recoup some of our funds?"

Eyes glistening, Harriet nodded. "I would be honored, Pastor."

"I'll clean things up before you start. I've been very remiss."

"Nonsense. Let me arrange the office to my liking. You can take care of the sanctuary." Harriet smiled. "It has always been a labor of love for me; I just took on a little more than I could handle."

"I am humbled by your generous giving of your time and deeply sorry that I paid so little attention."

"Apology accepted. Now eat your sandwich." Harriet grinned.

"Perhaps someone could cut the pie and dish it out, so I'm not the only one feasting. I believe I saw some paper plates and plastic forks on one of those shelves."

"I know where everything is. I'll do it." Harriet stood and efficiently prepared plates of pie, and Marge set them around the desk. "I keep bottled water in this fridge, too." Harriet handed one to Greg.

He reached for it with a smile then suddenly turned his head and called, "Come in. The door's unlocked," when he heard a timid rap on the door. Millicent opened the door and stepped inside, surprised to find not one but four people present. "I hope I'm not intruding."

"Not at all. Will you have a piece of this lovely pie Harriet brought?"

"Is it homemade?"

"No, you're safe." Harriet laughed.

Millicent grimaced. "I'm sorry, dear. I shouldn't have asked."

"Maybe you can teach me how to bake a delicious pie. I've heard yours are legendary."

"I would love to. It has been quite some time since anyone asked me to bake a pie. I find it very therapeutic."

Marge was quiet. *Harriet has changed, and so has Greg. Your plan might work, after all, Lord. She would make a perfect pastor's wife.*

"Marge?"

"Sorry, Joey. Did you say something?"

He laughed. "Several somethings, but the last one was you have pie on your nose." He handed her a napkin.

Millicent pulled a chair over next to Marge and sat down with her pie. Leaning toward her, Millicent whispered, "I was actually looking for you. I have some news I wanted to share, but you weren't home."

"I'm glad you're here. Would you like to come over for dinner?"

"Yes. That sounds lovely. What are we making?"

"I don't know yet." Marge winked.

"What do you think, Marge?" Pastor Greg asked.

"About what?"

"About planning a big fundraising event."

"By myself?"

"No! I wouldn't ask that of you. What kind of event could we host?"

Marge thought for a moment. "We could have a winter festival and ask the Catholic congregation to participate.

A tree trimming contest, sleigh rides for the kids, a pie-eating contest, turkey dinners and refreshments for sale, a Christmas sing-along or karaoke competition, a best Santa contest, a small train ride, everything with small entry fees and donated prizes. We can advertise at churches in neighboring towns too."

"Brilliant! Maybe some of our talented congregation could donate handmade gifts for sale; the kind we make for the town festival, but with a Christmas theme." Millicent grinned.

"Do you want to be in charge of the planning, Harriet?" Greg asked.

"No, I will help, but I don't want to be in charge of everything anymore. I need to leave a little time for creating friendships and possibly sleeping. I think Marge and Millicent should spearhead this one."

"I wouldn't know where to begin." Marge looked at Joey with panic in her eyes.

"Millicent and I will help. I bet she's a master." Joey patted Marge's hand.

Nodding confidently, Millicent said, "I am. I have plenty of experience."

"We should probably head home. James said he would stop by this afternoon, and we are interrupting your project, Pastor."

"I'll stay and work on the office if you don't mind."

"That's fine, Harriet. We can walk home. It's not far."

"Speak for yourself," Millicent frowned. "If I keep spending time with you, I'm liable to get fit, and who ever heard of a fit grandmother?"

"It will keep you feeling young, grandma." Joey chuckled. "You've seen what she puts me through."

Harriet looked at them with wide eyes.

"Get your mind out of the gutter, young lady. They do yoga on Facetime every morning."

"And we tried to sign up for Aikido, but the school is always closed when we go over there."

"I know Nakamura sensei. His class schedule is based on students he hopes will join rather than the ones he actually has, so you might have to ask him if you can start with a private lesson. Perhaps Harriet and I can join too, so he has four students."

Staring at Greg like he had grown an extra head, Harriet asked, "You're volunteering me for martial arts?"

He lowered his eyes and mumbled, "I just thought maybe we should find some common interests that aren't church related."

"But I don't know anything about martial arts."

"Neither do I, but it might be interesting to learn. It's a beginner's class, isn't it, Joey?"

"Yes. Nakamura sensei said it's okay for any age or fitness level."

"I'll think about it," Harriet said. "Now, let's get to work." She stood and began collecting forks and plates. "I'll take the pie over to the rectory and put it in the refrigerator." When Marge followed her outside, she said, "What does that mean? He said we should find common interests outside the church. He's never said anything like that before."

"I think he might be seeing you in a different light but proceed with caution. He is on the rebound."

"Oh, my. Take this pie. My hands are clammy, and I might drop it."

⋅⋅⟜⟞⟝⟜⋅⋅

Finding Joey and Millicent waiting outside when they returned, Marge said goodbye to Harriet and joined them for the walk home.

"That was very interesting," Millicent commented, and Marge had to agree. "Did he report the theft to the police?"

"No, but I did." Joey's lips formed a thin line.

Millicent nodded. "Good for you."

They walked in silence for a few minutes, then Joey squinted at a figure pacing in front of his house. "Who is that, Marge? You see better than I do."

"I think we should visit the eye doctor."

"Perhaps." As they got closer, he recognized Seth by his floppy hair and his youthful clothing, and he waved.

"I always think it's so awkward waving to someone and knowing they are waiting for you, staring at each other, and being unable to speak as you approach."

"I think so too. Sometimes I pretend I don't see them until I get closer, but it doesn't really help," Millicent said.

"I'll come over after I have a chat with our young friend," Joey said, veering to the right and crossing the street.

"See you soon," Marge called. "We can prepare dinner while you tell me your news," she told Millicent, unlocking the front door and tripping over Fluster, who was weaving around her legs and complaining loudly. "Poor baby. You're hungry, aren't you." She knew better than to pet him when he was in such a mood and headed for the pantry.

Millicent watched in amusement. "I've never had a pet. Why did you pick a cat rather than a dog?"

"I didn't pick him. He picked me. One day, before I met Joey, I took a walk to the town green and sat in the grass, enjoying the sunshine and looking for four-leaf clovers. Fluster came and sat next to me. He rubbed against me, climbed into my lap, and began to purr. He was just a kitten, so tiny and sweet. Sitting there, petting him, I wished he was mine, but I suspected he had a home somewhere and that he would remain in the park when I left. I set him in the grass when I got up and told him I had to go home, but he gave a pitiful meow and looked so sad, then he followed me as I walked away. When I reached the sidewalk, I was worried he would get run over, so I crouched down and said, *Are you all alone? Do you want to come home with me?* He tried to climb my pant leg, so I picked him up and snuggled him. I put up posters and asked around, but no one claimed him, and he's never shown any inclination to leave."

"Why did you call him Fluster?"

Marge laughed. "I was used to living alone. My home was quiet and orderly, but then he showed up and caused quite a commotion. Kittens have a lot of energy." Marge shook her head and smiled. "Fluster and Joey changed my life. I was just a kooky old schoolteacher, and that is still true, but now I've found my tribe."

"I want to be part of your tribe," Millicent said earnestly. "Even with the murders and all the upheaval in my life, I have felt so happy and alive since I came to stay with you. That's why I wanted to move here, to be part of the tribe."

Marge hugged her and smiled. "You already are." She let go and stuck her head in the freezer. "Now, what is your news?"

Chapter 33

Millicent sat at the kitchen table and paused. "I had a long conversation with Elizabeth, and she asked me not to move. We talked about why I wanted to move, and she agreed to make some changes. She even asked if I would show her the house I was considering. After we went to see it, she said she could understand why I liked it and asked if maybe we could create a cozy suite for me, with plenty of room for having friends over."

"I'm impressed. That doesn't sound like the Elizabeth I know. She seems to be really listening and considering your needs. Have you made a decision?" Marge had taken out a family-sized frozen lasagna and put it in the oven when it beeped and was starting a salad.

"I'm not being very helpful." Millicent walked over to the counter where Marge was chopping.

"That's okay. You can make coffee if you like. I'm interested in your story."

Walking over to the coffee maker, Millicent began filling the carafe with water and continued. "I like her idea, and she really does seem to be turning over a new leaf. I might buy the house down the street anyway if the owner lowers the price. I got the estimate from my contractor, and it's not as much as I thought it would be, but I haven't heard back from Christine."

"Why would you buy the house if you're not going to move?"

"I could try living by myself while the renovations are taking place and have a serene place of my own in the summertime, where we could barbecue and play in the pool, and if I decide I don't want to live there, I can always rent it to some nice family who needs a place to live."

She finished adding coffee grounds and pushed the start button.

"That sounds reasonable, and Elizabeth would know that you have a place to go if she doesn't hold up her end of the bargain."

Millicent grinned. "That too. I have one other piece of news. Let me get that." She headed to the door, but Joey had already let himself in, accompanied by Seth Drake.

"Hello, Millicent. I brought company."

"Your timing is good. I was about to share my second piece of news, which has to do with Seth's father. Come on into the kitchen."

Marge had finished the salad and poured three cups of coffee. "Have a seat. Do you drink coffee, Seth? Or would you like a soda?"

"Soda, please," he said quietly.

Marge served the beverages and sat with the others.

"I've been thinking about the milk plant and decided to ask James Nelson and Oliver Drake to run it together. I offered them salaries equal to what Reginald was earning and am giving them each ten percent ownership. They will be able to participate in board meetings and profit when the company profits. They both accepted."

Seth looked troubled. "Why would you give part of your company to a man who was fired for stealing and the father of your son's murderer?"

Millicent put her hand on his and smiled gently. "James is not a thief. He was fired unfairly for reporting Reginald's theft. And your father is a good man. He's not to blame for Sally's illness."

Hanging his head, he mumbled, "She always took care of me. I don't know what I'll do without her."

"She'll be back once she gets well. Maybe you can stay with me now and then," Joey said.

"I feel like a burden."

"Nonsense. I need help around the yard, and you need a place where you can have company and regular meals."

"Another member of the tribe." Marge grinned.

"You really don't mind?"

Fluster rubbed against Seth's ankles, and Marge laughed. "Look at that. Even Fluster is looking forward to your company. Just don't bring Carter over here because he might not be quite that forgiving."

They all glanced at Fluster's skinny tail, and then the oven timer beeped. Marge stood and removed the lasagna. "It will be ready to cut in about ten minutes. Would you like to come upstairs and meet Fergus?"

Seth stood. "Who is Fergus?"

"You'll see." She smiled and led him out of the kitchen.

<hr>

When they returned, Seth said, "Aunt Marge has a mouse! It's so cool!" His green eyes were glowing with excitement, and Joey smiled. "And she said I can take Aikido classes with you guys!"

"I didn't even think of that. Millicent, you should come too. Nakamura sensei is a friend of Pastor Greg's and trying to get his school up and running. He said Aikido can be done at any age or fitness level."

"I don't know. That sounds difficult."

"Let's at least try it," Marge said, cutting the lasagna. "It's purported to improve flexibility and balance, and it can't hurt to learn some self-defense moves."

Looking at Seth's glowing face and remembering Marge's words, Millicent said, "I'll give it a try... for the tribe."

Marge grinned and handed her a plate of lasagna. Once everyone had been served and the salad placed in the middle of the table, there was another knock on the door, so Marge went to answer it. Peter stood on the stoop, hat in his hands. "Do I smell lasagna?"

"You do. Would you like to join us?"

He grinned sheepishly. "Yes!" He followed her into the kitchen and stopped suddenly, surprised. "Good evening, everyone."

"What are you doing here?" Seth asked.

"Marge is my aunt. What are you doing here?" Peter raised an eyebrow.

"She's my aunt now too." Seth took a big bite of lasagna.

"What if I don't want to share?"

"Too bad. She's cool. She has a mouse."

They all laughed.

Peter joined them at the table and said, "The reason I'm here, besides dinner, is because the chief asked me to thank you and Joey for your help on the case. He also said that he didn't want you getting involved with any other cases." Peter kept his eyes firmly on his plate.

Joey laughed. "He says that now."

"What other cases?" Marge asked. "Nothing ever happens in Buckwood."

"Just like no one ever visits you unannounced?" Peter got up to answer the door, returning with Pastor Greg and Harriet, who was holding a pie.

"We have news and brought dessert. What smells so good?" Harriet looked toward the stove.

"Are you hungry? I have some extra chairs in the bonus room. Could you give me a hand, Seth?" Returning a moment later with two chairs, Marge invited her two most recent guests to have a seat and brought more lasagna. "It's not homemade, but at least it's family sized. What kind of pie did you bring, Harriet?"

"I found out this afternoon that Greg's favorite pie is lemon méringue, and luckily, that is one kind I am actually good at."

"Wonderful. And what news do you bring?"

Harriet smiled at Pastor Greg. "You tell them."

"I received a check in the mail today with a note of apology. Angelica returned the church money. I went straight to the bank to cash it and returned it to the church account."

"Did she give any explanation?"

"No. It's a miracle," he said, his eyes looking suspiciously moist.

"Good enough," Millicent's eyes sparkled. "I think we should go ahead with the winter fundraiser, though. When Pastor Greg followed the path God created for him, we all learned some very valuable lessons about faith, love, and community. Let's not ignore what we've learned."

"I'm relieved that the money has been returned, but I will never forget what all of you did for me, how you rescued me in my darkest hour."

"You have your flock; Marge has her tribe. Those of us who are extremely blessed belong to both."

"Here here," Joey lifted his fork. "Let's have pie."

Alice Kanaka has been reading everything she could get her hands on since she could hold a book and writing stories about the world around her. Her youth was a series of moves across the United States, accompanied by her sibling sidekick and her books.

After studying abroad in England and Spain and a short stint working for Club Med, Alice packed her bag once more and went to teach in Japan. Her story continues along the same vein, adding languages, kids and cats into the mix. Open one of her mysteries to see the world through her eyes. You won't be disappointed.

HTTPS://AliceKanaka.com

If you'd like to see more of Alice's adventures, make sure to check out her **travel blog!**

https://ExploringWithAlice.com

Sign up for Alice's mailing list to get notifications and to be entered in a monthly raffle!

<u>Coming Soon:</u>
Bumfuzzle and Cattywampus: Unlikely Detectives, Book 2

www.ingramcontent.com/pod-product-compliance
Lightning Source LLC
Chambersburg PA
CBHW020033310726

48970CB00007B/2234